See early No. of New Story in " Boys of England.'

" I will avenge him !" vowed Young Wildhawk, as the Brigand wiped his sword.

"Ralph Wildhawk, or Alone among the Brigands."

JACK HARKAWAY AND THE SECRET OF WEALTH.

CHAPTER I.

FLYAWAY GAP.

AFTER travelling fourteen days into the interior of the Black Hills, Jack Harkaway and his party came to a lake.

It was early morning.

The snow, which had fallen heavily during the past week, had disappeared under the influence of a sudden and rapid thaw.

Still, the air was cold, wintry, and biting.

The sun, which appeared for only a few hours a day, had no power of warmth.

Jack had ridden on ahead, closely followed by Harvey.

Half a mile behind came the waggon, drawn by four horses, and filled with valuable stores.

This was guarded by Ghost-that-lies-in-the-Wood and twenty-five braves of the Sioux nation.

There were two invalids in the waggon.

One was Professor Mole, who never walked when he could ride.

The other the eccentric travelling English nobleman, Lord Mossbunker, who had met Jack among the Indians and had the misfortune to lose his two ears, or "eaws," as he pronounced the word.

In addition to these two, Hilda, Harvey's wife, was accommodated with a seat in the waggon.

She was tired of riding.

Hank Smith, the scout and hunter, proved a splendid teamster.

Behind the waggon came Monday, Harkaway's black servant, and Hopkins, the English peer's valet.

A broad expanse of water lay stretched out before Harkaway and Harvey.

But in the lake, about a mile distant from the shore, was to be seen an island.

This appeared to be of considerable extent.

Away inland was a range of hills, perhaps fifteen miles off.

They were extensive, and so high as to almost deserve the name of mountains.

Harkaway's heart beat high.

"Dick," he exclaimed, "here's a lake, and I can see an island in it.

"And a pretty big island too," said Harvey.

"Who knows," continued Jack, "that this is the island in which the Mountain of Gold is to be found?"

"Very likely."

"You remember the prophecy of the old, dying Indian woman?"

"Mir-a-ma?"

"Yes."

"Of course I do. She said you were destined to solve the mystery of the island in the lake, discover the golden secret, and a lot more of the same sort."

"It seems to me it's going to come true," said Jack.

He let the reins fall on the horse's neck, and taking his opera-glasses or binoculars, from the case which was slung over his shoulder, levelled it at the island.

Suddenly he uttered a cry.

"What new discovery have you made?" asked Harvey.

"The island is inhabited."

"How?"

"It is, indeed."

"By mud-larks, perhaps."

"No—by human beings."

"Indians?"

"White men," replied Jack. "There is a settlement on this island, Dick."

"Impossible."

"Why?"

"We should have heard of it, if it were so," replied Harvey.

"That don't follow. It has all along been a mystery to know what became of the Black Hill miners who were disturbed and driven away by the United States troops."

"Well?"

"I'll bet they have come here to this retired spot, and, having found gold in the creek running into the lake from the hills, they are working it quietly and keeping their own secret."

"It is possible."

"Why, certainly," answered Jack.

Suddenly they were conscious there was some one near them.

A man emerged from some swamp-land and slouched along, with his hands in his coat-pockets.

He was roughly but not raggedly dressed, had on thick-top indiarubber boots, and a felt hat with a broad brim.

His countenance was swarthy, his hair dark, but he was clean-shaved and his hair cut short.

This indicated civilisation and luxury.

Moreover, he was smoking a cigar.

" Good-day, boss !" he exclaimed, staring at Jack, familiarly.

" Good-day," replied Harkaway.

" Where do you hail from ?"

" Nowhere in particular. I came here to explore this region in search of gold.

" Miner ?"

" Not a practical one."

" Got any stamps ?"

" A few."

" Are these your people behind ?"

" Yes."

" Do you want to come to the settlement ?"

" You have ask i me a good many questions. May I be permitted to put a few to you ?" said Jack.

" Sail in," replied the man.

" Who are you ?" began Jack.

" S anish Joe."

" What do you do for a living ?"

The man chuckled quietly.

" Most anything." he replied.

" Do you mine ?"

" Sometimes find a nugget, sell it, and then loaf till I want more greenbacks."

" Then there is gold here ?"

" Plenty of it."

" What do you call this lake ?" asked Jack.

" Ain't got no name, that I know on."

" Is the island named ?"

" No more than the lake."

" What's this settlement you speak of ? "

" Flyaway Gap."

Why did they call it that ? "

" You aint posted. It's easy to see that," said Spanish Joe.

" I am not."

" Well, you see, when the troops interfered with the miners, lots of them went home ; but there was some who wouldn't be beat off. Men who had invested their all in coming to these hills and brought their wives and families along with them."

" Yes "

" These penetrated further into the interior and reached this lake. They made rafts to serve as ferry-boats, and crossed to the island, which they took possession of."

" Call it the Island of Refuge," said Jack.

" Good for you ! They settled down over there, staked out claims, and called the place Flyaway Gap."

" Is that so ?" said Jack.

" Yes, sir."

" And they found gold ?"

" Plenty of it in the creeks flowing from the hills."

" How do they live ?"

" Oh, there's plenty of game, and sheep, and deer. We've had ice lately, though it's just broken up, and we could cross the lake without any trouble."

" How many people are there at the Gap ?"

" Going on five hundred men, women, and children," answered Spanish Joe.

" They require something more than meat to live on."

" They do, and they get it."

" How ?"

" We've established a pony express between the Gap and Cheyenne City, and we have every fortnight a train of waggons coming with provisions and all sorts of stores.

" Aren't you afraid of the troops finding you out ?"

" Our friends in Cheyenne don't give us away."

" Do the Indians trouble you any ?" queried Jack.

" Never seen a redskin here yet," replied Spanish Joe.

" How did you build your houses ?"

" We had axes and lumber in plenty. Our houses are all frame-work shanties, but they're good enough."

" Have you stores ?"

" Yes- all sorts."

" Can you sell your gold ?"

" We can. All we have to do is to go to a dealer. He'll take it at so much an ounce. Pay in currency, and then we have a high old time at the liquor-saloon."

" You've got a saloon ?"

" Half a dozen of them."

" Doing well ?"

" Roaring trade," replied Spanish Joe.

" How long have you fellows been here ?" continued Jack.

" Close upon nine months, and more keep on coming with the waggons every fortnight. I tell you, Flyaway Gap's going to be a big place."

" If the soldiers don't rout you out."

" Let them try it on," replied Joe. " We're armed, the hull on us, we mean to show fight before they land on our island, and don't you forget it."

" Can I and my party settle with you ?"

" Don't see any objection."

" Who's the boss of the Gap ?"

" Ain't get none. We're all bosses."

" How do you preserve law and order ? "

" We've got Select Men, and if a robbery or a murder is committed, we just form up into a Vigilance Committee, and settle the thing right slick out of hand," replied Joe.

" Rough and ready," said Jack.

" That's it to a T. Do you want to know any more ?"

" Yes. How do you cross ?"

" On the ferry-rafts. We've got two of them."

" Where are they ?"

" Half a mile to the south'ard."

" Is the island large ?"

" I guess it is, but none of us have prospected the other side of the hills as yet."

The waggon began to near the lake-shore.

Spanish Joe eyed it curiously.

" Got any chewin'-bacca to spare?"

" Yes," replied Jack.

" Any rye?"

" Yes."

" Well, I guess I'll take some," said Joe, coolly.

" At a price," replied Jack.

" What d'yer mean?"

" You'll have to pay for it," said Jack. " We don't give anything away.

" Who are you?"

" Jack Harkaway."

" Well," said Spanish Joe, squirting out some tobacco-juice over the horse's flank, " you're an all-fired mean cuss, and I'm sorry I've wasted time in talking to you. Guess I'll skip. So long."

With an air of disgust he turned on his heel and walked off.

" Why didn't you give him something?" asked Harvey.

" Because I don't like the fellow," replied Jack. " He's a dirty loafer, I'll bet all I possess. If we are going to stay among these people I don't want them to think they have got a soft thing in us, and play us for suckers, because we are not working miners like themselves.

" You're right." said Harvey, reflectively. " But shall you stay with them?"

" Yes."

"Why n t?"

"He'll skin you."

Old Ebony regarded Joe with an injured air.

"What do you want to crab this deal for?" he asked.

"Because you would'nt trust me for my rye the other day."

"You see," explained Blackwood, "I run a store and sell 'most everything."

"I understand," said Jack. "Locate us at once, if you will."

Joe saw that his attempt to injure the money-lender, storekeeper, dealer in gold, etc., was a failure.

He turned away with a curse.

Old Ebony regarded the Indian with surprise.

"Indians!" he exclaimed.

"Yes," said Jack. "Do you object to them?"

"We did't bargain to have any of those cusses here."

"Why not?"

"They might go and tell others where we are situated."

"Not they. I'll answer for them.'

"Well, it don't matter, I reckon" said Blackwood. "If they show themselves ugly, we've got lead for them. This is a peaceable community, stranger, and the one who raises a bloody muss has to swing for it, without having much time to say his prayers."

"Quite right too," answered Jack.

Blackwood conducted them to a spot about a mile distant from the settlement.

It was on the banks of a creek.

This creek was known to wash down gold from the hills, and the miners having claims on it could dam it to a certain height and raise out the dirt, which they afterwards ran through a sieve, and, using quicksilver, separated the gold from the dirt.

Blackwood apportioned them about two acres of land, received his fee of twenty-five dollars, and departed, wishing them success and a good time.

That night they camped as usual.

But when day broke they were all astir.

There were plenty of trees in the neighbourhood, and taking out their axes they cut down a quantity.

These were cut into logs, under Hank's direction, and in less than a fortnight six houses began to show themselves.

The Indians worked hard.

Only Mr. Mole and Lord Mossbunker showed a disinclination for labour.

But they had to do their share.

They were told that every man had to build his own house or sleep on the bare ground.

"What a howid countwy?" said Lord Mossbunker. "I'll go to a hotel. This is the sort of thing no fellah can suffah long and live."

But the Indians had taken all his money.

Even if he had been able to find a lodging at a saloon in Flyaway Gap, he was unable to pay for his board.

So he reluctantly set to work with Hopkins and cut up logs.

It had been hard work for all.

Whatever they wanted they had been able to buy in the Gap.

It was lucky they had money and stores with them, or their condition would have been most deplorable.

At length all were comfortably housed.

The weather, fortunately, had been mild.

The severe frost and snow of December had been followed by a moist rainy January.

When Jack saw that all was finished, and that his friends were protected from the elements, he shouldered his rifle.

"I'm going out for an hour or two, Dick!" he exclaimed.

"Going far?" asked Harvey.

"No; just a walk of five or six hours. I want to explore."

"All right," said Dick. "Be good to yourself. I think I shall take a sail on the lake."

"What in?"

"Oh, there's a dug-out canoe with a sail at the Gap I can get for a couple of dollars, and I may knock over some wild fowl."

"If you do, I'll dine with you when I come back."

"Go d enough!" exclaimed Harvey.

Jack light his pipe and sallied forth.

An hour afterwards, Harvey walked down to the village, hired the roughly-made canoe, hoisted sail, and with his fowling-piece at his feet, skimmed the placid waters of the island lake.

CHAPTER II.

HUNSTON AT WORK

BY a singular chance, the island that Harkaway and his friends had reached was the very one on which Olalla, the Corpse-maker, and Hunston were staying.

Therefore, Jack, without knowing it, was on the same island with his wife and child.

The wife he lamented as dead.

The child that he thought lost to him, perhaps for ever. On the other side of the range of hills of which we have spoken, not more than thirty miles off from Flyaway Gap, the Corpse-maker, Hunston, Viola, Young Jack, Jerry Post and his amiable wife were living.

Hunston grew very tired of his forced inactivity.

He wanted excitement.

At length he determined to take a bag of provisions with him, and, rifle in hand, go and make a circuit of the island.

It might take him a week.

It might occupy two.

He did not care.

Anything for a change.

So he prepared some food, filled his pouch with cartridges, and, loading his rifle, announced his intention of going on a tour.

Viola stopped him as he was leaving the camp.

it ? where is Harkaway ?"

"Short distance from the Gap."

"Mining ?"

"I don't think he is," replied Spanish Joe. "They have been building houses. The fellows are well fixed, I guess. Fact is, I didn't cotton to him worth a cent, and I've never been up to see how he and his friends are getting on. None of my business."

"Certainly not."

Hunston was afraid to attack Harkaway himself, as he had too many friends about him.

He thought he would engage Spanish Joe to kill him.

The idea flashed through his brain like lightning.

He would not tell him all his scheme then; he would take a night to think over it, and go and see him at the saloon he had spoken of as the "Crow's Nest."

He lighted his pipe.

"See here, Spanish Joe !" he exclaimed. "I mean business with you."

"Good enough. I've been unlucky at mining, and like my booze too well to miss a chance of making money," replied Joe.

"Will you get rid of a man for me ?"

"Who is he ?"

"I'll tell you and explain all when we meet."

"When will that be ?"

"To-morrow."

"You'll come and see me ?" said Joe.

"Ye-a."

"That's all right. I'll be either at the 'Little Brown Jug' saloon or at the Crow's Nest."

"I understand, and as far as £50 goes I'm ——"

"Don't talk about terms now. We can settle all that when we meet."

"I'll pay if you'll act," said Hunston.

"That settles it," replied Joe.

"So long," said Hunston.

"Be good to yourself," replied Spanish Joe.

Hunston did not deem it prudent to enter the town, as he might be recognised by some of Harkaway's party.

He retired into the woods, found a hollow tree into which he crept, ate some dried meat, drank some water from a rill, and smoking his pipe, gave himself up to meditation.

It seemed impossible to capture Harkaway in the midst of his friends.

So Hunston decided to go and hire Joe to kill him.

He secretly admired Viola, and thought if he could prove that her husband was dead, he might induce her to marry him.

It would be a good plan to hire Spanish Joe to drown Jack in the lake.

The dead body would float ashore, and people would think he had accidentally met with his death.

As for Young Jack, Hunston made up his mind to shoot him.

"I will have the father killed," he said to himself, as he sat in the cavity of the tree, smoking his pipe. "I'll shoot the cub, and then I'll marry the widow. When I'm tired of her charms, I'll throw her off and go to England. My two brothers will be avenged, I shall have cleared off the viper's brood, and I can settle down to work with an easy conscience and a quiet mind."

This was his villainous plot.

But he had to discover that rogues and villains never enjoy peace of mind.

haunts them.

In their hearts they have a canker.

It is like the worm in the bud.

The worm that gnaws continually and never dies until the victim dies with it.

In their souls is the fire that is never quenched.

Hunston, however, slept well that night.

In the morning he wandered through the woods and amused himself by killing a bear.

In the afternoon he strolled along the shore, and shot some wild birds.

Cutting off some bear-meat and preparing the birds, he had a dinner which gave him ample satisfaction.

Then he started for Flyaway Gap to seek out Spanish Joe and make arrangements with him to capture Harkaway and drown him in the lake.

CHAPTER III.

THE CROW'S NEST.

IN the newly-built settlement of Flyaway Gap was a place which went by the name of the Crow's Nest.

It was here that Spanish Joe lived.

He had received his nickname from his associates on account of his morose and vindictive temper.

He never knew much of his parents.

Those who did not like him—and there were few who did—said he had Spanish blood in his veins, which accounted for his cognomen.

Spanish Joe had done dirty work on more than one occasion, and had given his employer every cause to be satisfied with his execution of the orders he had received.

His terms were not extravagant.

Rowdies, as a rule, generally work in couples.

Spanish Joe's friend on all important occasions was a dapper little fellow called Gosh.

How he had acquired so singular a cognomen, it is impossible to say.

It might have been his father's before him.

It might have been given him at the font; but he always, when appealed to, declared that he knew nothing about it.

Every one called him Gosh, and as the principal party interested—namely, himself—did not object to the name, he was never spoken of except as Gosh.

This little man was wonderfully agile.

He was celebrated for climbing, and could jump over almost anything.

Both Spanish Joe and Gosh were fond of good living and drinking

Near the Crow's Nest was a saloon called the "Little Brown Jug."

This was a place of fashionable resort with the Crow's Nesters, who passed much of their time within its hospitable precincts.

Instead of going into the Nest, Hunston pushed open a door of the saloon and looked around him.

His entrance caused quite a commotion among the community.

They thought, most probably, that he was a stranger in the land, and that it was their duty to take him in.

A dozen or fifteen men were grouped near the bar, drinking sundry beverages of a fiery and potent nature.

Their faces were bad faces; and a physiognomist, such as Lavater, gazing at them with critical acumen and professional interest, would have shuddered, while being amused.

These twelve or fifteen men were, in their own proper persons, distinctive types of the criminal classes.

That man, with the shaggy eyebrows and bushy beard, with a scar on his left cheek, with the full and bulging lips, the flat nose, the low forehead, is capable of committing a murder, if he has not, in the course of his varied experience, done so already.

The one to his left, undersized, with the whining voice and the hypocritical leer, is a sneak-thief, and so on.

Amongst the dozen men there was not one who possessed a redeeming property, or one good soul-saving quality.

This assemblage was the rank foliage and the luxuriant fruit of the State.

They were jail-birds and gallows-birds to a man.

Hunston's gaze lighted on one individual with a loud voice and a coarse way of speaking.

This was Spanish Joe.

He beckoned to him, and the fellow obeyed the signal with alacrity, saying—

"Glad to see you, boss."

When the gang to which he belonged saw that the new-comer was a friend of Joe's, they resumed their conversation, and no longer made an ocular butt of him.

It was a rule amongst the fraternity that the watch, purse, and pocket known to anyone of their number should be sacred.

Had it not been for this salutary regulation, it is not too much to say that Hunston would not have left the Jug with a cent in his possession, or a coat to his back—so lawless and predatory were the men amongst whom he had been rash enough to venture.

"We cannot talk here," replied Hunston. "Have you no quiet place to which we can go where we shall be undisturbed and enjoy comparative freedom?"

"You can come to what I calls my apartments, squire," said Joe. "There's only my friend Gosh there. He's keeping house, because he's too drunk to get up, and small blame to him, seeing we went to a friendly meet two nights ago, and he took more than he could carry. This way, squire; follow me."

Hunston did as the ruffian requested him, and entered a house, externally in a tolerable state of preservation.

Joe stopped at the first floor, saying—

"Here's my diggings, squire. I can't abear going upstairs; it tires my legs and breaks my back."

He kicked a dirty-looking door open with his foot, and disclosed a scene of hideous untidiness which was a near approach to dirt and squalor.

Upon the floor before the fireplace lay the man he had called Gosh.

He had contrived to roll over on his back, and in that position he snored with a vehemence that was really startling—no porcine creature, in all the agony of an enormous and unnatural accumulation of fat, could have made more noise.

The floor was uncarpeted, the ceiling black with dust, and the fleckering flare and smoke of candles; cobwebs abounded in every corner, containing such huge spiders that a timid person would have shrunk away, fearing the venomous bite of a tarantula.

Upon a common, clothless deal table in the centre of this apartment stood sundry cans, which had, in hours gone by, contained ale, if it was fair to judge from the stains upon the wood.

These were flanked by glass bottles, which had contained whisky.

A couple of blankets lay in a heap upon a mattress which was on the floor.

Some dirty water stood in a basin, which was placed on a chair, for want of a washstand.

Several pieces of broken pipes lay about in all directions.

This was the apartment which the fellow, borrowing a slang phrase, spoke of as his diggings.

Spanish Joe walked up to Gosh, and, kicking him in the ribs, cried—

"Now, then, wake up, old Go-to-bed!"

Gosh growled and moved an inch or two, afterwards snoring as profoundly as before.

"This noise won't do. I must put a stopper on this performance," continued Joe, coolly taking up the basin of dirty water and throwing it over his friend's head and shoulders.

Gosh sprang to his feet with a startled air, and, sitting down on the edge of the bed, wiped the dirty water from his eyes with the back of his hand.

"Ha, ha!" laughed Joe. "Thought it was Niagarar coming down on you, didn't you? You was a driving your pigs to market a leetle too fast. I've got a genelman here. Wake up, and show him some of your civility."

"What did you want to go and do that for?" said Gosh, in plaintive accents. "You've made me that wet I don't know how to move myself."

"It won't hurt you. It's likely to do your complexion a world of good. It is not often that you and fresh water meet together. Now, move yourself. The genelman and me's going to have a palaver. Clean yourself down a bit and ask the genelman for a dollar. Then go to the Jug and get some whisky. Talkin's dry work."

Gosh grumbled in a subdued manner at intervals, but did as he was directed.

Hunston gave him the money, and he departed on his errand.

"Now's your time, sir. It's a clear field and no favour. You can talk your hardest, and no one but me to listen, and I'm bound to."

"The job I have for you is not by any means a difficult one. I want a man put out of the way."

Spanish Joe drew his finger across his throat, and looked inquiringly at his employer.

"No, no, not that, exactly; I shall not tell you to halt at that, if it is absolutely necessary. I have made a sort of half-promise that no blood should be spilled, and I was thinking, as the man lives near the water, you could take him some distance from land and drown him. It will be a quiet way of transacting the business, and one which will, I think, be preferable to violence."

"We'll do it, squire, and glad of the chance. Things are rather dull with us just now."

"We!" repeated Hunston. "Whom do you mean by we?"

"Gosh and myself. Gosh is him as you see mugging of it before the fireplace. We alway work together, and there is not a better follow, when sober, in all the gang, than Gosh."

"You can trust him?" said Hunston, doubtfully.

"Trust him, eh? I'd trust him with untold gold, or my life, either," replied Joe. "Oh! I know my man. We've been pal for more than fifteen years on and off. Both Gosh and myself have been 'sent up' for short terms, but we have never been separated long for a time; and he always says that if I get copped he'll do something desperate to follow me. Though we should both of us be sorry to leave the Crow's Nest, the air of which agrees with our complaint wonderfully well."

"Do you think the Mountain of Gold is on this island?"

"I do."

"Any way, we can but try for it."

"I shall be glad to get into winter quarters," said Jack. "We'll have more hard weather yet. We will go some little way out of town, stake out our claims and build our houses. Hank will teach us how, and then we'll search for gold. We have money enough to keep us, and we can buy things at the stores in Flyaway Gap. Do you agree with me?"

"Perfectly."

"I'll hold a council when the teams come up," continued Jack.

He had not long to wait.

The Indians halted.

Ghost-that-Lies-in-the-Wood joined Jack, as did Hank Smith.

"Where are we now?" he asked.

"That's more than the cap. knows, I guess," said Hank.

"This is Lake Unknown," replied Jack. "That island over there is the Island of Refuge, and that town you can see on its southern shore is Flyaway Gap."

"Population like the lake," said Hank.

"How?"

"Unknown."

"I beg your pardon. At the last census it was five hundred," replied Jack.

"Where did they come from?"

"Columbia, the true"

"What are their colours?"

"The red, white, and blue."

"By Gosh, kernel, you know everything. How is that?" said Hank, perplexed.

Harkaway told him all he had heard from Spanish Joe.

"It's good enough for us ter cast anchor thar cap.," said Hank.

"What do you say, Ghost?" asked Jack.

"I'm of the same opinion," replied the Indian.

"Carried!" said Jack. "We will move on to where Spanish Joe said the ferry-raft was, and go over, so as to locate before dark."

"I'll teach yer how t build log huts," said Hank, "and we'll be all fixed in a month. All yer'll want ter buy will be blankets and flour, to make bread ; and ef we can't do the rest, why, my life's been spent in vain on these perairies."

"I have every confidence in you, Hank," replied Jack. "And we will make a nice little settlement of our own."

"That's it."

"We may have to stop here twelve months."

"I don't care a cent how long it is."

"It is particularly fortunate, in my opinion, that we have struck this out-of-the-way settlement, and I think it will lead us to gold."

"Ter gold?"

"Yes."

"I hope ter goodness it may, and perhaps we'll do ourselves some good, ef the troops don't come and boot us out of our ranche. I can wash dirt as well's any man going."

The waggon had stopped, and Lord Mossbunker looked out.

"Hopkins!" he cried.

"Yes, m'lord."

"What are you standing there like a fool for?"

"Very sorry, m'lord," said the valet.

"Tell me why we are—a—stopping—has the—a—beastly cart got stuck in the—a—mud again?"

"No, m'lord. Come to water."

"Water, eh?"

A sepulchral voice in the waggon said—

"I don't want any of that"

It was Professor Mole.

He had been "heavy on the rye" since he said he had a bad leg and got put in the waggon.

"What do you think they want to come to wataw for, eh?" continued Lord Mossbunker.

"Can't say, m'lord."

"It's vewy odd that they can't steer us bettaw than that. I shall have to get out and walk and diwect them."

"You jest shet right up!" exclaimed Hank.

"My worthy fwend," replied Mossbunker, "I was not addwessing my wemarks to you. Howid countwy, where a man cannot speak to his own—a—servant without being inte—a—wupted by the —a—vulgaw common people!"

"Shet up, or I'll put a head on yer."

"I was not aware that I was deficient in that —er—article."

The snarl between the hunter and the nobleman was cut short by Harkaway.

"Forward!" he exclaimed, "and follow me."

Touching his horse with the whip, he sped along the shore of the lake to look for the ferry which the hardy and adventurous settlers had established.

Meanwhile, Hank started the team.

The waggon rumbled along.

Ghost-that-Lies-in-the-Wood led on his well-armed and thoroughly disciplined Indians.

The news of their arrival at a settlement rapidly spread through the little community, and all was excitement and expectation.

Lord Mossbunker was delighted.

So was Mole.

So was Hilda, who had experienced quite enough of travelling.

She, woman like, wished to be at rest.

In an hour's time they reached the ferry, and found the man with his raft.

He agreed to take them over for a stipulated sum, and the waggon being driven on board from the landing, the whole party embarked.

It was a slow journey.

All the men had to help in propelling the raft.

There were long poles which they used as oars working them against posts on the raft, and so laboriously sending the raft across.

It was a relief when they came to the landing at Flyaway Gap.

A curious crowd had collected to witness their arrival.

Spanish Joe had his own boat, which was a sort of dug-out.

He had been out wild-duck shooting, and had met with some success.

No one greeted them on their arrival.

It seemed to be nobody's business to welcome them.

But there was no objection made to their coming.

One man, however, who called himself the land agent, accosted Jack as he stepped ashore.

"Glad to see you, stranger," he said.

"Thank you," replied Jack.

"Guess you want to settle?"

"That's so."

"I'm land agent here. Bullion agent. Gold agent. Name of Blackwood. Do a large business. I'll stake you out a claim for twenty-five dollars."

"Very well," replied Jack.

He was among strangers, and thought it advisable to close with this offer.

Spanish Joe was standing close by.

"Bully for you, Old Ebony," he said.

stand? I will pay you for your trouble. The man at present is living here."

In a short conversation, Hunston made Joe fully understand whom the man was, and that he was to go to the Harkaway settlement.

The man, who was tolerably intelligent, listened particularly to these instructions, and promised the next day to put Jack out of the way.

Hunston gave Spanish Joe a sum of money, and took his leave of him, quitting Flyaway Gap at once.

Going some distance along the shore, he waited for a few days before he inquired the results of his villainy.

He was afraid that Harvey might recognise him if he staid in the town.

CHAPTER IV.

THE SUCCESS HUNSTON'S PLOT MET WITH.

SPANISH JOE was acquainted with Harkaway, as we know, he having met him on his first arrival on the lake shore.

Consequently, he would have no trouble in recognising him when he saw him.

Joe started with Gosh on his errand.

His first care was to find a boat.

This was not difficult.

An enterprising settler had started a saw-mill on the creek, and, lumber being plentiful, he supplied the inhabitants of the Gap with all the boards they wanted.

Among so many men, there was a variety of talent.

One had been a boat-builder on the Schuylkill, and he made boats.

There were several riding at anchor, or drawn up along the beach.

As Spanish Joe did not own one, and was not acquainted with anyone who would lend him one, his only resource was to borrow one and chance the consequences.

He selected a commodious little yacht, with a mast, sail, rudder, and a large locker aft.

"Get in," said Joe. "We'll take a fly up the lake, and beach her a few miles round that point, where we shan't be seen."

"All right," was Gosh's reply. "Off she goes."

The two men got into the boat, and sailed in the direction indicated by the leader.

Neither of them understood much about boating.

If a sudden squall had come on, the odds are they would have been capsized.

They beached their boat, and were about to spring ashore and go to the new settlement in search of Harkaway, when they were accosted by a man walking along the sands.

With a secret delight, Spanish Joe recognised the very man they wanted.

"Stand by," he whispered.

"Why?" asked Gosh.

"Here's the bloat."

"By gum! that's fine!" said Gosh, sharing his companion's joy.

"Is that boat for hire?" asked Jack. "If so, I'd like to go for a sail."

"We'll take you along, boss," said Joe, "for the sum of five dollars."

"I'll give it you," replied Jack.

He stepped on board.

Jack saw he was in a trap.

He could not imagine what the motive for this outrage was.

Fearing he would be murdered, he begged them to spare his life.

The two ruffians whom Hunston had employed to drown him totally disregarded his appeals.

They laughed at his entreaties, and spurned his prayers.

A life was nothing to them, and they regarded blood as worth little more than water.

The boat steadily pursued her way, and the scoundrels took no notice whatever of the prisoner.

They laughed and chatted with one another.

The settlement soon receded from view, and became a mere speck in the distance.

A rocky shore was visible on either side of them.

But straight ahead, nothing was to be seen except a vast expanse of lake.

Suddenly it struck Spanish Joe that the time to commence operations had arrived, and turning to his companion, he said :—

"I don't think we can do better than begin here. We are some distance from land, and after drowning the bloat we can run the boat ashore, land ourselves, and let her drift till she breaks to pieces. It will appear then that we didn't know how to manage the boat, and that she has been wrecked with the loss of all on board."

"That will do," responded Gosh. "You could not have made a better plan."

"No one will blame us," continued Spanish Joe. "So you see, we shall do our work well, and earn our money."

Jack had listened to these remarks, and had been able to understand them.

It was clear to his comprehension that the two men who had embarked on board the boat had made up their minds, for some purpose or other, to kill him, and he said to Spanish Joe :—

"Don't kill me! What have I done that you should wish to take my life? I will do anything you wish me, if you will not drown me."

"Who talked about killing or drowning you?" said Spanish Joe. "We only want to teach you how to swim. It will be useful to you some day. It is not cold, and you will find the water nice and comfortable, and—come over here. Look alive, my man, far the time is slipping by, and we must be thinking of getting home again."

"Oh!" cried Jack. "You wish to kill me, I know you do; but the curse of Heaven always overtakes murderers, and it will sooner or later overtake you."

"We'll stand our chance of that," replied Joe, with a laugh. "All we want you to do is to get ready for you bath. There's no snarks about, so you need not be alarmed."

Jack threw himself down in the bottom of the boat.

If his hands had only been unbound, they would not have talked to him as they did.

"Oh! that is your little game, is it?" exclaimed Joe. "We will soon have you out of that. Come here, Gosh, and lend a hand."

Gosh did as he was directed, and Jack was soon struggling impotently in the grasp of the murderers.

He cried out as loud as he could, but the wind carried away his cries mockingly, and the fickle away."

Lily did as she was requested, and went away casting upon him a look of compassion, which made him hope much from her good nature.

She had not been gone long before the door of the dungeon again opened.

A rustling was heard, and by the light of the lamp carried by Josiah Redlynch, Harkaway, to his extreme astonishment, beheld Mrs. Cabuchon.

She wore a look of exultation on her face, and her manner was that of a woman who had triumphed.

Waving her hand to Josiah Redlynch, Mrs. Cabuchon told him to withdraw.

"But," she added, " stay within sound of my voice, in case I should need your aid."

Redlynch bowed in an awkward fashion, and retired into the passage, leaving the ponderous door ajar.

Harkaway, guessing this woman to be the cause of his imprisonment, regarded her sternly, and crossing his arms over his breast, waited for her to speak.

" Jack," she exclaimed, "I have come here to ask you for the last time whether you have any inclination to make me the reparation I require for the insults you have heaped upon me?"

"I am not aware," he replied coldly, "that refusing to return a woman's love is to insult her."

Mrs. Cabuchon shook her head, while a sad smile played about the corners of her mouth.

"Ah!" she said, with a sigh, "it's the bitterest of all insults."

"If you so interpret it," he replied, "you must blame yourself. I have nothing to regret. I have examined my actions, and I can find nothing to reproach myself for."

"What?" cried Mrs. Cabuchon, indignantly. "Is it nothing for a man to tell a woman she may hope, and to suppose she may be the favoured object of his choice?"

"Do you say that I did that?" he answered, casting down his eyes.

"I do say it, and repeat it, and being a high-spirited woman, I will not allow myself to be trampled upon, and have my softer and holier feelings crushed with impunity."

"I wish to hold no further conversation with you," replied Harkaway.

"But being my prisoner, and detained here at my pleasure, I do not see how you can very well help yourself," answered Fannie. "So long as I choose to speak to you, so long must you be content to listen."

Harkaway sat down moodily upon the straw, and unable to turn away his gaze from Mrs. Cabuchon's sparkling eyes, which fascinated him with their passionate expression.

"I have come here," continued Fannie, "to offer liberty—life."

"On what condition?"

"You know the condition well enough. Do not pain me by compelling me to name it. It is not well for a woman to woo a man."

"I will spare your blushes," said Harkaway. "The condition is one that is impossible for me to consent to."

Her eyes flashed like those of a tigress.

"Think well," she said.

Then it occurred to Harkaway that he would be justified in promising this woman anything, if by so doing he could gain his liberty.

"How can love and persecution exist together?" he asked.

"The latter is the result of the former," she answered.

"I consent to your terms!" he exclaimed, at length.

"You will make me your wife?"

"I will."

"That is well. Are you prepared for the immediate celebration of the ceremony?"

"The immediate celebration?"

"Why not? I am not disposed to trust a man who has behaved as you have done. A priest waits my call up-stairs. He shall come down here and go through the sacred rite.

"In a population like that of Fyaway Gap, all trades, callings, and professions are represented, and I have found a man who has been a priest."

"In this vault?"

"Certainly."

"It—it is sudden," stammered Harkaway.

"Ah!" cried Fannie, becoming furious. "You have lied to me. Now you shall feel the effects of my resentment—die in this dungeon! Your friends shall never know what became of you."

Jack hesitated again.

In that hour of supreme trial he was sorely tempted.

The temptation to accept the proffered hand of the lovely and accomplished woman who stood before him, and who would have been transported with joy at his affirmative answer to her appeal, was very great.

But the image of his dead Viola would arise up before him, and he felt that he was pursuing a right course in being faithful to her memory, though death, immediate and painful, were the result.

"Jack Harkaway," continued Mrs. Cabuchon, "I leave you to your fate."

"Have you no pity?" he asked, with an imploring glance.

"Have you any pity upon me?" she answered. "Why should I liberate you? No, no, no! You shall die! I will blot you from my memory!"

"God forgive you!" said Jack.

Fannie lingered for a brief space, as if she hoped that he would relent; but finding he was firm in his purpose, she said—

"If you should change your mind within the next four-and-twenty hours, a message will bring me here instantly. Good-bye—perhaps for ever."

"Yes—for ever," he answered, mournfully.

With a look in which love and hatred were strangely mingled, Mrs. Cabuchon took her departure, and Harkaway was alone.

So fierce was his longing for liberty, that he got up and was on the point of calling his visitor back.

Thoughts of Viola restrained him.

Though tempted again, he was true to his love.

It was with great difficulty that Jack kept any account of time, but about ten o'clock at night, as near as he could judge, he was favoured with an unexpected visit from Lily Redlynch.

"Hush!" she cried, laying her fingers on her lips to enjoin silence.

"It cannot yet be morning," he said.

"No, it is not yet midnight. I have come to warn you that your fate is decided upon, unless you consent to marry the lady who came to see you this morning."

"Would they murder me?" asked Harkaway, who trembled violently.

"Anywhere, so long as you leave this place, and are never seen around any more."

"Is that the decision?"

"It is."

"I have acted wrongly," said Fannie. "I am a wicked woman, and perhaps it would have been better for me to die."

"Oh no! Life is sweet."

Fannie's tears fell fast.

"How I loved that man!" she continued, "and how cruelly he has treated me! But I will forgive him, and begin life again."

"Promise me you will not try to injure Jack again."

"Must I swear that?"

"Yes, indeed."

"Well, you have my promise. It shall be as if he did not live. He need not fear me after this. Goodbye, dear, and believe me, my eternal gratitude is yours."

Fannie's face became hard and cold.

She was like a statue chiselled out of marble.

"Are you going?"

"Yes."

She pressed her livid lips against Hilda's cheek and walked out into the dark night, first drawing her hood over her head.

Where she went, or what became of her, nobody knew.

She was not seen or heard of at the Gap.

There was despair in her heart, and remorse was gnawing her mind.

Hilda felt sorry for her.

She saw desperation in her eye, and said to herself—

"Poor thing! She will not live long."

The next day the waggon was packed with stores, and the camp broke up.

Mr. Mole had been down with the fever, and was very weak and ill.

They put him in the waggon as well as Hilda.

Hank, as before, was teamster.

Jack, Harvey, and Monday walked together in advance of the waggon.

Their determination was to push for the hills, which they intended to thoroughly explore.

But they did not know that every step they took brought them nearer to the spot where Olalla and Hunston were encamped.

Jack's heart would have beat faster had he been aware that he was decreasing the distance between himself and his beloved wife and child.

Startling adventures were before them.

Their party seemed more comfortable, now they had got rid of Mrs. Cabuchon and the Indians, and since Lord Mossbunker and Hopkins had left them.

They heard the eccentric specimen of nobility and his faithful servant had left the Gap for Cheyenne City by a mule-team going that way, his intention being to return to his beloved London as soon as possible.

On the third day out, Jack camped at the foot of a large hill, which was one of a chain or series of small mountains.

There was every indication of this being a rich gold region.

A few days' prospecting would decide this.

. . . .

When allowed to depart from the backwoods settlement, Fannie wandered purposely towards the shore.

The silver moon shone upon her pallid face, and the far-off stars shed a golden radiance upon her beautiful hair, which, all dishevelled, flowed over her neck and shoulders like a cascade of the precious metal.

Sitting down upon a rock she fixed her eyes upon the sand, and listened to the murmuring waves as they washed the beach at her feet.

She was very miserable.

Her passion for Jack had been entirely crushed now, and she felt that she could never love him again.

All she had to live for was revenge upon him, but that she could never hope to obtain, as her wickedness had been discovered, and she had promised Hilda as the price of her liberty that she would never injure him again.

This being the case, her career was at an end.

Without money and friends, what could she do?

We know that Fannie was a woman of resolution and daring, or she would not have followed Cabuchon to the Black Hills to avenge her injuries.

He was dead, and had fallen beneath her hand.

She thought, as she sat there all alone asking herself what the wild waves of the lake were saying, that it would be best for her to die.

It very often happens that strangely emotional women like Fannie give way to despair.

A person of impulsive nature and hysterical tendencies is more likely to commit self-murder than the easy-going one, who takes things as they come, and allows nothing to disturb the even tenor of his way.

The grey dawn of morning was now breaking in the east.

Rising from the rock, shivering with cold and staggering like one who had been drinking, she neared the sea.

Her intention was to cast herself into the sea, find a lasting repose in its cold embrace, and throw herself on the mercy of her Creator.

Poor, erring, wayward spirit! She was more sinned against than sinning, and had she married a different man to Cabuchon, her fate might have been altered.

But her life was broken and mis-spent, as the lives of many of us are, through no fault of our own.

The cold and calculating, the mean and the narrow-minded, often succeed where the generous natures are borne down and crushed out of sight, in the wild whirl of busy life.

Raising her hands to Heaven, and accompanying the gesture with a glance skyward, she prepared to plunge herself beneath the waves.

Oh, what a depth of agony that poor pale face revealed, with its livid lips, its glazing, lack-lustre eyes, and the quivering muscles, which too plainly told the tale of heartfelt suffering!

One moment more, and the rash act would have been consummated.

Her suicidal intent was arrested by a loud cry—

"Hold on, there!"

She started back, alarmed to find that her privacy in that early hour of the morning was intruded upon by anyone.

Had it not been so, Fanny Cabuchon would have soon been a floating corpse, a mere lump of inanimate clay, over which not one word of Christian burial had been said, tossed to and fro like so much lumber, on the heaving bosom of the lake.

But God willed it otherwise.

Looking seaward, she could see nothing but the sun rising in a burst of golden splendour.

pany with the ruffians

They headed their boat towards the settlement.

"How did you come to meet with those villains?" asked Harvey.

"In the simplest manner possible," exclaimed Jack. "You know I went out for a stroll."

"Yes."

"I got to the lake shore, and thought I would like a sail, these fellows had a boat drawn up on the beach, and I asked them if five dollars would pay them for taking me out. They said it would, and I jumped in, but scarcely had my foot touched the boat than I was knocked down and bound."

"Then they put out to sea!" exclaimed Harvey."

"Exactly."

"What was their object?"

"I can't tell."

"Robbery?"

"No. They didn't offer to take a cent from me," replied Jack.

"Why should they attempt to murder you?"

"That's what I want to know."

"Have you made any enemies at Flyaway Gap, since we have been here?"

"Not one that I know of; we've been too busy building to go into the town, and so came in contact with no one."

"That's so!" exclaimed Harvey, thoughtfully.

"It's a mystery to me," continued Jack. "I'll be hanged if I can make it out at all."

"Nor I."

"But there's one thing about it, and that is, I owe my life to you. If you had not been taking a sail, I should have gone up."

"Ah, pshaw! What does that amount to? You may save me to-morrow. In these parts, we hold our lives in our hands."

"I think I know one of the fellows," said Jack.

"Do you?"

"Yes. I have a good memory for faces."

"I know you have."

"Well, the boss villain was, as well as I can place him, the man I first spoke to when we came to the lake."

"What is his name?"

"Spanish Joe."

"We'd best keep an eye on him."

"You bet I will, though that shot of yours will keep him quiet for a while, or I'm much mistaken."

"I meant it too!" exclaimed Harvey, with a quiet laugh.

They soon beached their boat, and returned across lots to their home.

It being more convenient, they all messed together in Hank's house, and Monday and Hopkins prepared the food, and waited on the table.

Supper was ready on their arrival, and while engaged in eating the meal, they forgot the exciting adventure they had just gone through.

CHAPTER V.

THE CHARCOAL-BURNERS.

THE two ruffians found their plans defeated and their designs frustrated by the most singular accident that had ever befallen them.

They could not blame themselves for it, because perpetrate.

They resolved to renew their efforts on a future and more auspicious occasion, and dismissing the incident from their minds, considered how they might best hide themselves for a while.

They were afraid to go back to the Gap at present.

Spanish Joe's leg pained him very much, and though it did not bleed excessively, the shot which had lodged in the flesh caused him exquisite torment.

He had gone into the wood in order to avoid the kind attention of the Select Men, and both Gosh and himself wandered on in a purposeless manner until they lost themselves.

The wood into which they had unguardedly penetrated was of great size, as far as they were enabled to judge, and they began to despair of finding any path.

It was growing rapidly dark, for during winter there is little or no twilight.

At length Joe, thoroughly wearied out, sank down at the foot of a tree and declared he could go no farther.

His leg gave him a twinge as he bent it to assume a sitting position, and he screwed his face into such a ludicrous shape that Gosh exclaimed, with a laugh—

"Don't do that, mate, without you want to make me to die of laughing. You look as ugly as a sack full of monkeys."

"I wish I was back in the Gap again, and in the bar of the 'Jug,'" replied Joe. "Bless that fellow for laming me like this. I'll be one with him, though, some day for it."

"Come, get up," said Gosh. "If you sit there till it's dark we shall have to make a night of it in this wood, and that's a thing I would rather avoid if I have the choice."

"I tell you I can't move," answered Joe, petulantly. "You go if you like. Leave your pal to die in the wood. That'll be a pretty story to tell, won't it?"

"No, my boy, I'll never do that," said Gosh, feelingly. "If it is to be a case of die, why, we'll go under together. I'll never leave you; though, if you feel equal to it, I should like you to show a leg and step out a little."

Spanish Joe, however, reiterated his asseveration of his inability to move.

So Gosh lighted his pipe, and sat down beside him.

Half an hour passed in silence.

Neither of the men spoke.

Gosh was sulky, and Joe was in too much pain to do anything but groan.

At last the darkness became profound, and Gosh, who was looking through the trees, perceived a light, which appeared to emanate from a huge fire.

Touching his companion on the arm, he called his attention to the discovery he had made.

"Perhaps we are near some shanty," he said; "anyhow, there must be human beings about. Wake up, Joe, and let's go and see what it is."

"I can't move," replied Joe, "my leg's so painful. You go and have a look. If there is any shelter, come back for me."

Gosh, accordingly, walked slowly forward until he arrived at the scene of the fire.

He stood behind the trunk of a tree and gazed

the interstices of which were filled up with clay, as a poor and feeble protection against the wintry blast.

Around a large fire were grouped two men, having a wild and shaggy appearance.

Their appearance was strongly indicative of Jewish origin.

Their beards were long and black, their locks shaggy and unkempt, their clothes dirty and ragged.

There was something weird and fantastic about them to Gosh, who had felt as Robinson Crusoe did when he came unexpectedly upon the kitchen-fire of the cannibals, who were cooking their dinner.

He had a good mind to run away, but curiosity restrained him.

While he watched, one of the men went into the hut and brought out half the carcase of a sheep. He put it down by the fire, and with his knife cut off a large piece, which he evidently intended for his and his friend's supper.

When he had accomplished this task to his satisfaction he took back the remainder of the mutton to the hut and shut the door carefully after him, as if he was fearful that some one would watch his movements.

These men called one another Shadrach and Bendigo.

They were charcoal-burners.

Charcoal was used at the Gap for purpose of gold-melting.

Their life was a savage one, and the sheep, a part of whose flesh they were about to devour, had been shot by them.

The night-air was chilly, and the ruffian was in a desperate condition; his friend was ill, and the fire of the charcoal-burners looked warm and enticing, so Gosh made up his mind to accost them and ask permission to bring his friend into their comfortable circle.

Stepping forward with this intention, he made himself visible and said :—

"I hope I see you, mates."

The charcoal-burners started to their feet on seeing a stranger, and exhibited symptoms of violent alarm.

Shadrach shouted hoarsely to Bendigo, and each seizing a blazing, spluttering brand, they stood upon the defensive, as if they expected an attack from the intruder, and were prepared to make one upon him.

Gosh retreated a step or two, as if in doubt how to proceed.

The charcoal-burners seemed to think that the intrusion upon their solitude meant them some harm.

Strange, wild-looking men were those charcoal-burners.

Their state appeared at first sight to bear a resemblance to the primitive or savage condition of men before the light of civilisation dawned upon the human race and raised men in the social scale.

Their long and shaggy hair, their twisted, matted, tangled beards, their dusky skins, tanned by exposure to the sun, browned by the attacks of inclement weather, and naturally of an olive tint, owing to their Israelitish blood; their dark, piercing eyes and their prominent noses; their ragged clothes, their strong frames, all combined to strike the beholder with wonder, if not with awe!

who had burst unceremoniously upon the privacy of the charcoal-burners

But Gosh was an individual who feared nothing, and when both men snatched up burning brands, with which to attack him, he followed their example, and armed himself with a log as big as a club all flaming, flaring and smoking.

With this upraised in his right hand, he stood upon the defensive.

Seeing that he was determined to resist, the charcoal-burners thought it would only be prudent to hold a parley with so determined a foe.

Accordingly, Shadrach exclaimed, in a gruff voice, which he had acquired by continued exposure to the weather:

"Who are you, and what do you want here?"

"I am a miner," replied Gosh, "and have lost my way in the wood. I don't mean you any harm. I have a friend lying at the foot of one of the trees yonder, who has hurt his leg, and if you or your friend will show us the way out of the wood, or give us shelter for the night, we will give you something for your trouble."

"He speaks fair enough," said Shadrach to Bendigo. "Shall we trust him, and do as he requests?"

"Ask him if he belongs here," replied Bendigo.

"Where do you hail from?" inquired Shadrach.

"Flyaway Gap."

The charcoal-burners once more conferred together, and the result of their deliberation appeared in Shadrach's reply—

"Go and bring your wounded friend. We will give you a share of our fire and some supper."

Gosh was overjoyed at the successful issue of what at first threatened to be a sanguinary adventure.

He could have fought one man for any length of time, but he did not feel himself equal to the task of encountering two men.

For the end of such a combat could not be long doubtful.

He would, in the nature of things, have been conquered in the course of time.

Joe was too much injured and too exhausted to be of the slightest use to him.

In five minutes he had retraced his steps, and was standing over Spanish Joe, who was groaning heavily, as if in great pain.

"Cheer up, old man," exclaimed his companion. We're in luck to-night."

"I'm blessed if I think so. What am I to do with my le ?" responded Joe, with a growl.

"I'll see to that presently. First of all let's go and have a good warm and a bit of something to eat."

"Don't be a fool and talk nonsense. I'm not in the humour for it," said Joe. "Where are we to find a fire, or anything to cook?"

"Not far off."

"Are you in earnest?"

"Of course I am," answered Gosh. "I happened, fortunately, to come across a couple of men burning charcoal They had half a sheep in their hut, and there is a most appetising smell of mutton-chops. Do you think you can get up and limp along with my assistance, or shall I carry you?"

"Let me lean on your elbow, and I am sure I can walk a short distance."

scene just in time to be of the greatest service to Hunston.

CHAPTER VI.

LUCK IS AGAIN ON JACK'S SIDE.

"WAL cap," said Joe, chuckling again, "ain't I fixed him dead to rights for you?"

"Indeed you have," said Hunston.

"And if I haven't killed him, haven't I earned the ducats?"

"That's so, Joe."

"You'll cash up?"

"Like a man. Got any cord?"

"Yes."

"Hand it over. I'll bind his hands and let him kick for a while, so's I can think what to do with him. Perhaps it wouldn't be safe to shoot him here, as he has friends around."

"I guess not, cap. Don't shoot," said Joe.

"Besides," said Hunston, "I've got other plans. I want him alive now, and I'll take him with me."

"That's your biz, cap," returned Joe.

He fumbled in his pocket for some cord, and eventually produced a couple of yards.

Hunston made Jack's arm fast behind his back. He let him lie on the sand.

Then he got up and glared at him as a tiger may at its prey.

"I'll lay him out with a stone, if you say so," said Spanish Joe.

"No, no, he's safe enough," said Hunston.

"Oh. jee! how my blamed leg does pain me!" continued Joe.

"Does it?"

"Yes, sir. I wouldn't have had that walk for less than a thousand pounds, if it hadn't been for Gosh, and my feeling so bad over his death."

"You didn't study me any, then?"

"Yes, I did."

"Well, here's your money," said Hunston, giving him some bills.

"Thank you."

"Now we're square."

"I'll bet you; and if you want anything in that line done again, you call——"

"Not on you," interrupted Hunston.

"Why not?"

"Because you bungled it."

"I did?"

"Yes. You made a botch of it," said Hunston.

"Wal, I'll allow I didn't drown him, but then, yer see, squire, that some people ain't born to be drowned."

"That's right enough."

"Got any booze with you, squire," continued Joe.

Hunston produced a flask of whisky, which he had purchased at the saloon when he was at the Gap.

"We'll wet this," said Joe. "I feel as if I'd done a big thing, and it's no use talkin', I can do it when I'm wanted. I didn't drown him, that's sure; but there's more ways than one of killing a dog."

"You scoundrels!" said Jack, "how dare you do this!"

Hunston smiled pitilessly, like an executioner.

"What are you going to do about it?" he asked.

Jack was silent.

What could he do

against odds."

He had been suddenly overpowered by Spanish Joe's attack in the rear, and was bound in a moment, being a helpless prisoner.

Hunston allowed him to sit up, and stood by with his arms folded, gloating over his misery.

"You thought you'd done a fine thing when you tracked me out here," said Hunston, tantalisingly.

Jack preserved a sullen silence.

"The trouble was, he counted me out, and thought I wasn't worth a cent on that deal," remarked Joe. "But when he shot Gosh my old and particular friend, my dander was riz, and I trotted after him in a way I didn't think my leg would let me. I'd sworn to lay him out, and that's a fact."

"My only mistake was in not killing you, too, my friend," answered Jack.

"That's my opinion, only the cleverest of us are liable to make errors sometimes," replied the ruffian, with a grin.

Hunston took some money from his pocket and gave it to Joe.

"Is that enough?" he asked.

"If you're satisfied, boss, I am," answered Joe.

"You can go."

"Don't you want me no more?"

"Not at present."

Joe drew a murderous-looking knife and flashed it in the sun.

"If there's any blood-letting to be done, I'm on hand," he said, significantly.

"Not now, thank you," answered Hunston. "If anybody kills this man, it will be me. I wouldn't sell that treat for any amount, and at present his life is safe."

"How?"

"I mean to take him with me."

"Where to?"

"That's my business. Do you see that boat lying off the Giant's Rock?"

"I do."

"Some fellow beached her there this morning, and I mean to take possession of her. Harkaway and I will sail together to the place I came from. So good-bye, Joe. I'm a thousand times obliged, and I shall know where to find you when I want you again."

"That's so, cap. You've paid me well, and I'll serve you well at any time. Oh, my leg! how it begins to ache again! I'd give something just to have a cut at somebody. It might let some of the savage feeling out of me."

He brandished his knife within an inch of Jack's face, as if he wanted to let him know who that somebody of whom he spoke was.

"I'm bad!" he exclaimed, "and it's no use a-talkin'!"

"Keep that bloodthirsty pirate away from me please," said Jack.

"He shan't hurt you," replied Hunston. "You heard me say that you were *mine*. Solong, Joe."

Spanish Joe turned to go.

Meanwhile Hunston's small frame was dilating with delight.

His triumph had come upon him so unexpectedly.

Now he could take Jack to Olalla's camp, confront him with his wife and child, and put

It took effect.

The bullet crashed through the villain's brains, and he fell to rise no more.

"That settled it," said Jack, grimly.

The noise of the firing woke Joe, who, with the aid of a stick which served him as a crutch, emerged from the shanty to see what was going on."

"Ha!" cried Jack again. "Here is another of them."

Having the murderous readiness of Gosh before his mind, he pointed his gun at Joe.

"Dont shoot, cap !" exclaimed Joe.

"Are you armed?"

"No, sir. Don't shoot."

"Down on your knees."

Spanish Joe sank on his knees.

"Hold up your hands."

He did so.

"Now," said Jack, "answer my question, or you will follow my friend."

"Ha—have you killed him?" stammered Joe.

"No doubt about that," said Jack.

"Is he dead?"

"Dead as mutton."

"What for did you kill him?"

"Because he fired at me first."

"Why should he fire on a stranger? That's very wrong of him"

"Ah, pshaw! stop that," said Jack. "You've got no pudding in me I suppose you'll say next you never saw me before."

"Never: so help me——"

"Don't tell lies," interrupted Jack. "You know very well that you got me on board a boat to kill me, and that my friend, Mr. Harvey, rescued me."

"No sir. You're mistaken in your man."

"Am I?"

"Yes, indeed, cap."

"It's the first time in my life, then, that I ever forgot a face. Stop this fooling, and tell me who employed you, or why you did it?"

"I've nothing to say," responded Joe.

"Say your prayers," said Jack.

"He raised his gun again.

"Don't shoot, cap," cried Joe, in an agony of fear. "I've got lead enough in me now to run a shot-tower Don't you do it."

"Own up."

"I will, I will!"

"What was your object?"

"We were paid to do it."

"Who by?"

"Some fellow. I don't know his name," replied Joe.

"Does he live at the Gap?"

"No, he doesn't I'm sure of that, for I'm always around, and know most, all the crowd."

"Do I understand that a stranger hired you to put me out of the way?"

"Yes, sir."

"I suppose, after you'd done the deed, you were to meet him somewhere?"

"Yes, sir."

"Where?"

"At the Giant's Rock."

"I don't know that place," said Jack.

"It's on the south beach, sir, about four mile out of the town," said Joe.

"When were you to meet him?"

"Any day I could get up when the sun was at its highest."

"Twelve o'clock you mean?"

"That was the arrangement, boss."

"Good enough so far. Now tell me what this man is like?"

"Young fair, not too stout, and wall-eyed."

"Blind of one eye?"

"Yes, sir."

"Hunston, by Jove!" exclaimed Jack.

"What's that you say, sir?" asked Spanish Joe.

"None of your business!" exclaimed Jack.

He had heard all he wanted.

It was strange that Hunston could be on the same island, and should have found him out.

If Jack had been wise he would have returned to his camp and taken the advice of his friends.

But he was angry and indignant.

It was only eleven o'clock.

He guessed he could walk four miles in an hour, and get to the Giant's Rock about midday, in time to meet this stranger who was so anxious to take his life, and whom he did not doubt for a moment was Hunston.

Without saying good-day to Joe, or bestowing a thought upon the dead man, Gosh, Harkaway strode away towards the sea.

He was very stern and grave.

Fully occupied with his own thoughts.

If he had killed Gosh, the latter had forfeited his life by trying to kill him.

This new attack of Hunston's showed how determined and pitiless the man was.

"He'll never let me alone," mused Jack: "like his brother, he must keep continually pegging away at me. This last attempt shows, too, what a coward he is at heart. Why did he hire assassins to kill me? Because he was afraid to do it himself."

He laughed a hard, metallic laugh.

"Yes," he added, "he must die, or I shall never know what peace is in this world. Why can't he let me alone? Do I interefere with, or interrupt him? The world is big enough for both of us. His hate towards me is like a Corsican Vendetta, handed down through generations. I must shut right down on this thing."

He walked through the wood, emerging on the table-land leading down to the sea.

Part of it was ploughed up, showing that certain of the colonists were about to raise corn and potatoes when the spring came.

But he thought little of agriculture just then.

The wavelets of the lake were rippling pleasantly up against the pebbly beach as he proceeded.

Almost before he was aware of it, the huge proportions of the Giant's Rock were looming up before him.

He halted abruptly.

A figure was leaning against the rough and jagged sides of the rock.

One glance sufficed to show Jack that he was in the presence of Hunston.

He advanced to meet him.

"Hunston!" he cried, while a fierce joy surged up in his breast.

They were both armed with pistol and rifle.

"How do, Harkaway?" said Hunston, affecting a friendly air.

"You dare to speak to me?" said Jack.

"Why shouldn't I?"

"Ask yourself."

"Ah, pshaw! let us be friends. Who'd have thought of seeing you here?"

Her voice, usually so soft and gentle, was hard and stony as she said this.

"Murderess!" he ejaculated.

"Do not call me that," she said, plaintively.

Jack's usually clear head was in a whirl.

The course of events since he had been at Flyaway Gap had been rapid and exciting.

He had met with Hunston, and he unmasked Fannie.

"Allow one thing, Mr. Harkaway!" she exclaimed. "At least. I have always been actuated by a desire to serve you."

"And yourself too."

"In what way?"

"You had a selfish end in view."

"Name it?"

"You wanted to be my wife."

"Is that a crime?"

"Yes. I am wedded to the memory of the dead, and you should know how to take 'No' for an answer. I hate this atmosphere of intrigue in which you delight to live, and I refuse to have anything further to say to you from this day forth."

Her expressive face flushed under the red skin.

"You seem to forget, sir, that I have just saved your life!" she said.

"I forget nothing."

"That man did not know me again, but I knew him."

"Whom do you mean?"

"Hunston, your sworn enemy, my late husband's friend. He would have killed you, had it not been for me."

"Where is he?" said Jack, for the first time thinking of Hunston.

The Indians had been attentive listeners to this conversation.

One of them, named Wild Goose, pointed to the lake.

"Gone," he said.

"He has escaped me," said Jack, much vexed.

"Yes, and only to strike again," said Fannie, now Ghost-that-lies-in-the-Wood no longer. "Surely you have need of friends, Mr. Harkaway."

"I have them," he replied.

"Can you afford to make an enemy of me?"

"I wish to make an enemy of no one."

"But——"

"My dear lady," interrupted Jack, "if I cannot ⟨be fr⟩iends with a woman without marrying her ⟨she will⟩ remain my enemy."

⟨She⟩ flashed indignantly.

"⟨V⟩ery well," she said, in a tone of concent⟨rated⟩ fury; "you have said enough, and more ⟨th⟩an enough. I cannot any more humble myself ⟨befor⟩e you."

J⟨ack⟩ made no reply.

H⟨e wa⟩s watching the boat which, swiftly skimming the water, was carrying Hunston far away, he knew not where.

Wild Goose had been talking to his friends.

Suddenly he spoke.

"Ghost-that-lies-in-the-Wood heap big fraud," he said. "Indians go home. Leave her. Sioux never followed a squaw. Ugh! that is bad."

"You can go!" said Fannie.

"How deceive Red Dog, Blue Horse?"

"Through Ira-pa-cap-ka. I met him by accident. He persuaded me to adopt this disguise, and introduced me as a travelling warrior to your chiefs."

"Why do this?"

"He knew my husband, Cabuchon, in the old days, and he hated him as much as I did."

"Heap bad. Indian go home. Feel small to be led by squaw. Ugh! the fool-killer been among Indians. Ugh! It is heap bad. Dam!"

Wild Goose and his warriors went away, leaving Jack alone with the Blonde Beauty.

That night all the Sioux Indians left Flyaway Gap and went home.

They had deserted the false chief.

All the influence of Ghost-that-Lies-in-the-Wood had vanished like a summer's dream when they learnt that "he" was a woman.

Looking at Jack, Fannie exclaimed:—

"My career as an Indian is over, but I suppose you will have no objection to my remaining a member of your party?"

"Shall you abandon your disguise?" he asked

"Yes. I will go and buy some clothes at the Gap, and dress more like a lady."

"You are welcome to stay with us," said Jack, "though, if I may suggest, you will act wisely in going with the first mule-team to Cheyenne City."

"What am I to do then?"

Jack shrugged his shoulders.

"I really cannot tell."

"A woman in my position feels it difficult to do anything," she said, bitterly. "I am without money, friends, or resources. Well, I must think what it is best for me to do, and for a time I will eat the bread of idleness, and thank you for it in my heart."

"Understand one thing distinctly, Mrs. Cabuchon."

"What is that?"

"I don't want you fooling around me any more than you can help. I have work to do here, and I must hurry up to find the Secret of Wealth."

"With me you might find the secret of happiness," she ventured to say.

"Bah! that is played out!" he exclaimed, impatiently. "When we meet I shall treat you with distant politeness. That is all."

"So be it," answered Fannie, with a laugh.

He strode angrily away, to return to the settlement.

Fannie did not remain long after him.

She took a look at the dead body of Spanish Joe, and started for Flyaway Gap, where, with the little money she had, she knew she could buy the necessary goods which would make her a woman in appearance once more.

Hot water would remove the red dye, a chignon would make her hair look nice, and she would be herself again.

But her heart was full of bitterness and rage.

She hated Jack for his contemptuous treatment of her.

Scarcely had she started to go than a man who, apparently, had been out duck-shooting, came up.

He had half-a-dozen couple in his hand.

"Thunder!" he exclaimed, "that's Spanish Joe's body. So he's got the lead at last, poor beast! I always thought he'd come to that."

Then his eye fell upon the Indian.

"Say, Injun, did you do this?" he added.

His face wore a threatening expression as he spoke.

"What if I did?" replied Fannie.

"If I thought so, I'd drop you in your tracks"

"You would be a fool for your pains."

"Oh! I'm a desperate man, and don't care a curse for anybody that crosses me."

A thought flashed across Fannie's mind.

away, and all your friends, at the—a—hotel, you know."

"Thank you."

"Except—a—that wude hunter man, and that black cutthroat whom you call by a—er—Weekday—let me see."

"Monday?"

"Yass, yaes; that is it. Except wude hunter and Monday."

"I should like to give you a send-off."

"A—pardon me—a what?"

"Sort of parting supper."

"Parting suppah? Vewy kind, I'm sure, but we can get all we want at the hotel, and as soon as my eaws are well, I shall go away to my own countwy, you know."

"Best place for you," said Hank.

"Hopkins!" said Lord Mossbunker.

"Yes, m'lord."

"What are you standing there like a fool for?"

"Very sorry, m'lord."

"Are my trunks packed?"

"Beg pardon, m'lord."

"Is the cab at the—a door?"

"Don't quite understand, m'lord."

"What time does the—er—twain start?"

"No train 'ere, m'lord."

"Oh, no, confound it! I thought I was at home. Well, good-bye to all of you. Come, Hopkins."

The pair took away a few skins belonging to them, and plodded back to the Gap, to stop at the Sharon House, which was a wooden shanty kept by an enterprising genius from Nevada, who thought he could do better for himself by selling bad rum than by washing red dirt.

. . . .

Fannie saw nothing of Harkaway, and only left her hut to visit Hilda in hers.

The men spoke politely to her, but forbore to make any remark upon the singular way in which she had been unmasked.

In the afternoon she kept herself entirely alone. She was awaiting the promised visit of Dartazzan.

He came at last.

There was a knock at the unpainted door.

"Mrs. Ghost—um beg pardon, Mrs. Cabuchon-that-Lies-in-the-Wood!" exclaimed the voice of Monday.

"Yes," she replied.

"Um heavy rooster come to inquire for you."

"What is his name?"

"Say him name of no consequence."

She opened the door.

It was Dartazzan.

She beckoned him in.

"Thank you," she said to Monday.

The Malay retired, and she closed the door again.

"Here I am on time," he exclaimed, "according to agreement. What do you want of me?"

"Will you capture a man for me?" said she.

"And kill him?"

"That depends upon circumstances."

"I'll do it for money."

"Here is all I have in the world," she said, placing some bills before him.

He counted them.

"Fifty dollars!" he mused. "Not much; but it's hard times."

"Will you do it?"

"Who's the man?"

"Harkaway."

Dartazzan started.

"They say he's a tough," he mused, "but I'll tackle him."

"Do so, and let me know the result."

There was another knock at the door.

"Who's there?" asked Fannie.

"Harkaway," was the reply.

She turned a shade paler.

"May I beg you to kindly wait a moment?" she exclaimed.

"Certainly."

There was an inner room, and, pointing to the door, she said, hurriedly, speaking in a low tone—

"Get in there. The very man we were talking about is outside."

"Who?"

"Mr. Harkaway."

"What is this?" asked Dartazzan, pointing to the door.

"A small closet. You will be safe there. Listen to our conversation, if you like, but do not come out till I tell you."

"Good enough."

"You understand?"

"Enough said."

Dartazzan entered the closet, and had scarcely done so than Fannie, opening the door, said —

"Come in, Mr. Harkaway."

Scarcely had Dartazzan ensconced himself in the convenient hiding-place which Mrs. Cabuchon pointed out to him than Jack Harkaway entered the hut.

Mrs. Cabuchon received Harkaway coldly.

"To what fortunate circumstance, sir am I indebted for the honour of this visit from you?" she asked.

"Mrs. Cabuchon," he answered, with a somewhat embarrassed air, "I feared that I had said or done something of an ungentlemanly nature."

"Not at all," she hastened to exclaim.

"I wounded your feelings."

"I was not aware of it."

"I rejected your advances."

"Sir!" she cried, angrily, "I made none to you; therefore, it is impossible that you rejected my advances."

"But——"

"You utter an untruth, sir, as often as you repeat that statement."

"Really, I do not know what to do. I came to beg your pardon, but it seems to me that I have done nothing to beg pardon for."

"Nothing."

"Absolutely?"

"Absolutely nothing," said Mrs. Cabuchon.

"Then all that remains for me to do is to wish you good-morning."

"Good morning," said Fannie, frigidly.

He moved towards the door.

Then a hope—a frantic, fierce, irresistible longing—that there was something more in his mind than he had given utterance to—that he came intending to tell her he loved her, and that he had changed his mind, rushed across her.

If so, she was guilty of great folly, for she was driving him away with the pent-up words unuttered.

As he reached the door, she exclaimed—

"Stay!"

"Did you call me?" he asked.

"I did. Have you aught else to say?"

"Have I?"

"Yes. Do not let me drive you away without an opportunity of making any explanations which you may feel it your duty to make," she said, in her turn becoming embarrassed.

"Oh, dear, no! I only came to apologise for any seeming rudeness, as I said before."

"And that is all?"

There was a lingering tenderness in her tone.

This, however, did not affect him in the least.

He was thinking of Viola, his lost wife.

"That was all," he replied, repeating his words.

As he went away, the last hope died out in her breast.

She saw that Harkaway never could be hers, and all the tigerish ferocity she had formerly displayed broke out in her pallid face and sat on her quivering lips.

Hastily opening the inner door, she clutched Dartazzan by the arm, exclaiming—

"You have seen him! after him—after him! Lose not a moment. He cannot have gone far. Go, go!"

"All right," answered Dartazzan, quickly leaving the room.

Alone once more, Fannie ran to the window, pulled aside the shade and looked out.

Jack had gained the edge of the clearing, and was walking leisurely along.

Like a grim shadow Dartazzan followed close behind him.

Inevitable fate was dogging the footsteps of the man she once loved, and whom she now hated with all the passionate force of a wicked nature.

Harkaway wandered on, he scarcely knew whither, all unconscious of the villain full of a deadly purpose who followed him.

Mrs. Cabuchon was a dangerous siren.

During the interview Harkaway felt more than half-inclined to be recreant to his plighted troth and sacred word of honour.

More than half-inclined to forget Viola, and avow a love, he scarcely knew whether he felt or not, for the beautiful Cabuchon.

Sometimes there had been a strange light in her eyes that he almost feared.

Jack determined to withdraw to the Gap.

He wanted to see a little life, in order to distract his mind.

A fog was rising from the lake and spreading over the low grounds.

Yet Dartazzan, with the unerring sagacity of an Indian who has struck a trail, never once lost sight of his victim.

Feeling fatigued, Harkaway leant against a tree, and lighting his pipe, stood musing.

On the whole, his love for Viola was more powerful than his admiration for Fannie.

He determined to be true to her memory.

And yet he was sorely tempted.

While he was ruminating, a voice at his elbow exclaimed—

"May I presume so far as to trouble you for a light, sir?"

"Certainly," replied Harkaway, turning his eyes upon the stranger.

Dartazzan—for it was he—lighted a cigar from the pipe which Jack Harkaway proffered him, and also leaning against the tree, said, in a friendly tone of voice—

"A strange place this Gap."

"Very much so," answered Harkaway, suspiciously eyeing him.

"What strange sights you see, and what strange people you meet!"

"Ye-es," replied Harkaway, still more drily than before.

"Now, I'll bet you'd never guess what I am by trade," continued Dartazzan, becoming, as it were, confidential.

"Well, No. I don't think I should."

"Guess."

"Impossible, my dear sir."

"Then I shall tell you. I am a bullion merchant, and when I add that I have several hundred dollars' worth of nuggets in my pocket at this minute, you may imagine that I place considerable confidence in you, or I should not make an admission about such valuable property."

Harkaway regarded him sceptically.

He took the fellow for a confidence swindler

"He is trying to impose upon me," he thought. "I have nothing particular to do for an hour or two, so I will amuse myself with him."

"I feel very much flattered, I am sure," he answered.

"Do you feel disposed to make a purchase? I can sell you something cheap," said Dartazzan.

"Not to-night, thank you. I'm not buying gold."

"Well, let us go somewhere to have a glass of wine. I can pay for a bottle, if you like."

Harkaway hesitated.

He was afraid of foul-play.

He feared that this man might have accomplices within call.

"Ah, I can see what is passing in your mind!" exclaimed Dartazzan, noticing his hesitation. "It is a peculiarity of your character that you have a mistrust of strangers. Perhaps you are right, but I can give you references. Oh, you may trust me. I am not the sharper you think me."

"I did not imagine that you were anything of the sort," said Harkaway. "But you must admit there is something odd about such a casual encounter as ours?"

"Willingly."

"Where shall we go? I will follow you, as I should much like to see your nuggets."

"Come on, then," replied Dartazzan, in a scarcely perceptible tone of triumph. "I will take you where you shall see some of the best specimens of the Black Hills."

CHAPTER VII.

THE HAUNT OF THE ASSASSINS.

DARTAZZAN had always been the associate of thieves and scoundrels of the blackest dye.

Like Spanish Joe, he had a daring and unscrupulous tool, who was named Josiah Redlynch.

Redlynch was a "body carpenter," or coffin-maker, as to his trade, and the most brutal and reckless ruffian who ever cursed the fair face of God's earth with his detestable presence.

Redlynch lived in the Crow's Nest.

In Josiah Redlynch's window a hideous-looking coffin was conspicuously placed.

But, in truth, he did not work much at his trade.

The coffin was placed in the window as a sign of his calling; but, as he often remarked, "chaps didn't die worth a cent at the Gap."

His best job was a stabbing affray or a shooting-fight.

Mrs. Redlynch, or Sally, as everyone called his wife, was a tall, stout virago of a woman, and, as the neighbours knew, a very dangerous antagonist in a drunken row, such being the congenial pastime in which she was superlatively fond of indulging.

It was to his friend's room in the Crow's Nest that Dartazzan, chatting gaily, took Harkaway.

Night had now fallen.

Jack did not suspect the new danger he had fallen into.

Three knocks, given sharply in succession, brought Sally Redlynch to the door.

Her red face was more than ordinarily flushed by her deep potations, and she scowled savagely at Harkaway.

But when she saw Dartazzan, the muscles of her face relaxed, and, winking at him, she exclaimed—

"Come in. We've been expecting you this ever so long. You'll find a nice fire in the stove."

The darkness of the night prevented Harkaway from beholding the ghastly emblem of the grave which formed the conspicuous furniture of the window.

Had he seen it, he might—frightened by so gloomy an omen—have been strongly tempted to forego the pleasure of making Dartazzan's acquaintance, and to have returned to his friends at once.

A strong smell of tobacco pervaded the atmosphere of the passage, which was more perceptible as they entered the parlour.

The apartment dignified by this name was very small.

In a chair sat Josiah Redlynch, smoking a pipe.

Before him, on a table, stood a can, nearly full of beer.

He got up and nodded as Dartazzan entered, and, looking curiously at Harkaway, exclaimed—

"Who have you got with you?"

"A customer. Light another candle, please. We shall not be able to see the red dirt to any advantage in this light."

Josh vacated the chair in Harkaway's favour, making a gurgling noise, resembling smothered laughter, as he did so.

"What will you drink?" asked Dartazzan of Harkaway.

"Nothing, at present, thank you," was the reply.

"Oh, you must have something. I have my reputation for hospitality to keep up. What shall it be—spirits?"

As Harkaway still hesitated, Dartazzan gave Sally Redlynch some money, and made her fetch some whisky.

He lighted a pipe, smoked and talked for some time both with Harkaway and Redlynch, but made no attempts to produce the nuggets.

Feeling uneasy, he scarcely knew why, Harkaway exclaimed—

"Will you oblige me by showing me the gold of which you spoke, as I wish to get back."

"I am very sorry," returned Dartazzan, politely, "but I find I have not them with me. I could get them, of course, by going to my own house. You would not, however, wish to inconvenience me to such an extent."

"I shall wish you good evening, then," said Jack, rising, "and the next time you wish to make yourself merry at anyone's expense, depend upon it you shall not do it at mine."

"Pardon me once more."

"For what?"

"I cannot allow you to go. The evening's entertainment is only just commencing. Pray sit down again," said Dartazzan, with all the equanimity in the world.

"I have already told you that I intend to leave this house, into which you decoyed me by false pretences," replied Harkaway.

"Harsh language," remarked ⟨illegible⟩ Red-

you both that I shall not allow myself to be robbed without making a desperate resistance."

Dartazzan put his hand into his pocket, and produced a revolver, which he extended at arm's length, saying—

"That is my answer to your threat."

The perspiration began to stand in beads upon Harkaway's face.

The intentions of these two men were only too evident.

He was in a den of thieves, assassins—he knew not what.

"My good fellows," he said "I wish to do you no harm; if you want my money and my watch, you are at liberty to take them. It is fitting that I should pay the penalty for my folly."

"Come, that's reasonable," said Redlynch.

"Yes," put in Dartazzan, "the gentleman is behaving in a sensible manner. Sit down, if you please, and place the contents of your pockets on the table."

Harkaway did as he was requested.

Soon there was a pile consisting of a handkerchief, a wallet, a pocket book, several letters and papers, two rings, and a watch and chain.

"Very nice, indeed," said Dartazzan. "Now, Josh, I leave the gentleman to you."

Redlynch at this rose from his chair, put down his pipe, swung his huge arms backward and forward, as if to get up the steam in his stalwart frame, and approaching the table, took a coil of rope which he held up to Harkaway.

"To bind you with, if you make any resistance," he exclaimed.

"What are you going to do with me?" cried Harkaway, in alarm. "Have I not given you all the valuables about me ? Do you want my life?"

"That depends," answered Dartazzan, coolly examining the make of his watch.

"On what?"

"Circumstances."

"I will pay you handsomely, if you will let me go."

"It strikes me we shall get more by keeping you," said Dartazzan, with a sly chuckle.

"From whom?" demanded Harkaway.

This speech caused a new light to dawn upon him.

"That's my secret."

"Ah! Mrs. Cabuchon. You are her spy—her agent—her assassin! I see it all now! Fool! Why was I not more circumspect ?"

"Take him away," exclaimed Dartazzan, waiving his hand. "He begins to weary me."

Without any ceremony Redlynch seized Jack by the collar and dragged him, in spite of his vigorous resistance, out of the room into the passage.

Here Sally Redlynch was waiting with a lighted candle.

"What a time you've been !" she said.

"Not long," answered her spouse.

"You ain't generally so long with them—that's all I know."

This speech filled Jack with a new terror.

It seemed to him that the people in whose power he was were professional cutthroats.

He had not much time for deliberation.

Sally Redlynch walked on, leading the way along the passage, down some steps, to a large chamber, which had the appearance of an ice-house.

It was damp and mouldy.

Rats scampered about in all directions as Sally Redlynch appeared with the light.

But whether human or not he could not tell.

He very much feared the former.

"There's your lodging," exclaimed Redlynch, throwing Harkaway on to the straw. "Make yourself as comfortable as circumstances will admit. I'll bring you something for breakfast to-morrow."

Slamming a heavy, iron-bound door to, Redlynch bolted it outside, and Jack was in darkness

Banished from the eyes of men!

Taken from the ranks of the living and the midst of his friends.

What Spanish Joe had failed to accomplish for Hunston, it seemed as if Dartazzan would perform for the Blonde Beauty, the vindictive Fannie.

"Can such things be?" he asked himself.

His own miserable condition was a sufficient answer to the question.

CHAPTER VIII.

IN THE DUNGEON.

WHEN Jack vanished again, Harvey, Mole, and the remainder of the little colony were at their wits' end.

They searched high and low for him.

Their efforts were fruitless.

A week elapsed.

All this time Harkaway was languishing in a noisome dungeon, into which the light of day never penetrated.

Why his captors spared his life he could not tell.

That they would continue to do so he did not dare to hope.

One day, when the door of the vault swung back, Harkaway was surprised to behold a very pretty girl enter with the customary portion of bread and the usual jar of water.

This was Lily Redlynch.

Strange as it may appear, the daughter of Josiah, and Sally, his wife, was as good at heart as she was lovely in the face.

Lily was obliged to obey her father and mother; and when she was told to attend upon the prisoner in the vault, she did so, though she wondered what the wretched individual had done to incur her father's resentment and be so incarcerated.

When she saw that he was a handsome young man, of gentlemanly manners and pleasing address, her sympathy redoubled.

"Ah!" exclaimed Harkaway, rising from the straw, "what vision of beauty mocks me? Are you some fairy come to set me free?"

"My name is Lily, sir," the girl replied, "and I am the daughter of Josiah Redlynch."

"His daughter? The child of that ruffian? Impossible!" exclaimed Harkaway.

"He is my father," said Lily, in a tone of reproof.

She knew Redlynch to be unscrupulous, but she was far from thinking him the atrocious scoundrel he really was

She did not know that he had stained his hands with the blood of human beings

Had she even surmised such a thing, she would have left his house for ever, risking the frowns of the cold world, and welcoming starvation, if no good fortune befell her.

"Oh!" exclaimed Lily, "I cannot see how my presence here once a day will alleviate your distress."

"My child," replied Harkaway, "I am loth to associate you with the villainy of your parent. Your coming here at all I look upon as a good omen. You will ask yourself who I am, and why I am here?"

"My father has told me," answered Lily.

"What has he told you?"

"That you are a bad man, that you attempted his life, and that he has taken the law into his own hands, and keeps you here in preference to handing you over to Judge Lynch."

Harkaway smiled.

"Is it possible, my child," he said, "that you can believe such nonsense as that?"

"I—I don't know, sir," she answered.

"Do I look like a would-be murderer?"

"N—no."

"Is there anything truculent in my appearance?"

"Not that I can see, sir; but if you are not what my father describes you, what are you?"

"I am——"

Jack Harkaway's communication was cut short by the stentorian voice of Josiah Redlynch, at the top of the steps, who exclaimed—

"Lily!"

"Father calls me. I must go," she said, tremulously.

"Farewell, my dear girl. We shall have an opportunity of speaking to one another on a future occasion," said Harkaway.

Nodding her head in token of assent, Lily tripped away, locking the ponderous door after her, and Jack was alone once more.

Alone with his misery,

But his misery was by no means so great and so unendurable as it had been.

He fancied he saw a possibility of working upon the sympathies of Lily Redlynch, and by such means contriving his escape.

Groping his way in the dark to the spot where the bread and water were placed, he made a heartier meal than he had done since his imprisonment.

The hope of liberty, though remote, sweetened his hard fare.

He waited anxiously for the next day, which would bring with it another visit from Lily, but whether Josiah suspected something, or whether it was merely caprice on his part, he came himself with the bread and water, which he deposited on the floor, just within the door, without saying a word.

Subduing his disappointment as well as he was able, Harkaway patiently awaited the coming of the morrow.

With it came Lily.

"I must not stop long," she said. "Father was so angry the last time I came; and were he to suspect that we were holding a conversation together, he would not allow me to visit you again."

In a hasty manner, Harkaway explained to her that he was Jack Harkaway, and that he had been enticed away from his friends.

At first Lily would scarcely believe this, and seeing that she was sceptical, he drew a handkerchief from his pocket, and tearing off the corner, handed it to her, saying —

"There is nothing I fear, that my father would hesitate to do for money," replied Lily. "I am ashamed to call him father, since I know the extent of his villainy."

CHAPTER IX.

THE ATTEMPTED ESCAPE.

"In what way am I to die?"

"You will be killed and dismembered here; a secret spring in the centre of the block which stands in the middle of the dungeon, causes it to revolve, and anything thrown down the hole which becomes disclosed falls into a creek which is only boarded over, and runs into the lake."

"Horrible!" said Jack.

"I implore you to marry the lady, and save yourself," said Lily.

"I cannot," he replied.

"Oh! what can I do?" cried Lily, in despair.

"Inform my friends of my condition; let my sorrowing friends know where I am, and all will be well," replied Harkaway, eagerly.

"My father! I cannot betray my own relations."

"They deserve their fate."

"The gallows would be their portion."

"What matter? You have done that which is right," said Harkaway.

"No, no. Were my father a thousand times worse than he is, yet could I not put the rope round his neck. I fear that cannot assist you unless you sacrifice your love, and consent to be the husband of the beautiful lady who has set her heart upon you."

"I have told her, and I tell you, I would sooner die," replied Harkaway, firmly.

"Oh!" said Lily, "if I had such a lover."

Such devotion struck her as approaching the height of sublimity.

It was grand and noble in the extreme.

"I must not stop," she said. "But I will see if I cannot get a chance of liberating you when father's back is turned. If he would only leave me the keys when he is absent, all could be accomplished."

Thanking her for her good wishes and kind promises, and exhorting her to do all she could for him, Harkaway, with reluctance, wished her good-night, and saw her quit the dungeon, of which he again became the sole tenant.

He tried to sleep, but in vain.

The chopping-block communicating with the creek haunted him.

Frightful visions floated before him in ghastly array.

After hours of terrible mental suffering, a deep perspiration broke out all over him, and he fell back, faint and exhausted, upon the moist straw.

* * * * *

Josiah Redlynch visited his prisoner, and intimated to him that recourse to final measures would be had unless he consented to the terms imposed upon him by Mrs. Cabuchon.

The pertinacity with which this woman urged her unmaidenly suit disgusted Jack.

"Tell her," he said, "that I will welcome death before dishonour."

"That is your answer?" said Josiah.

"It is."

"Sleep over it; and if you give us the same reply to-morrow, why, we must make short work of you. It comes expensive keeping people here."

"My determination will be unchanged," answered Jack, "and if you are bent upon murdering me, you had better despatch me at once."

"I'm agreeable," returned the ruffian, with a leer, "but must obey orders. Sleep over it, I say, and perhaps you'll change your mind. You might do worse."

Jack waved his hand impatiently.

The man's garrulity was very distasteful to him.

Muttering something about mules and obstinacy, Josiah Redlynch took his departure.

Jack fell back upon the heap of mouldy straw, which was by courtesy called a bed, and pressing his hand to his brow to still its throbbing, gave way to despair.

Unless he allowed himself to be conquered, the morrow would see him a corpse.

He was gone from the sight of the world in the most mysterious manner.

No light could be thrown upon his disappearance, and his body would be cast into some loathsome drain instead of having decent sepulture.

Raising himself from the state of stupefaction into which he was plunged, he commenced walking about the narrow dimensions of the cell in which he was confined.

Suddenly, in the dark, he stumbled against the block we have already described as resembling that used by butchers.

It stood in the centre of the dungeon.

Extending his right hand to save himself from falling, he caught hold of the block.

His fingers pressed something which seemed, from its coldness, to be brass.

Slowly the block revolved, in obedience to some hidden mechanism.

It disclosed an aperture.

This Jack was unable to see, but he knew that an opening was revealed, because a rush of cold, fetid air assailed his nostrils.

This was the secret of the prison-house.

After having killed and mutilated their victims, the assassins caused the block to revolve by touching the spring, and then cast the ghastly remains into the creek which ran beneath.

An idea occurred to Harkaway.

If he remained in the cell death was certain.

If he cast himself through the aperture into the well-like blackness beneath, and trusted to fortune, which might favour him, there was a chance of ultimate escape.

Yes, remote though it was, a chance existed.

What man in Jack's position would have refused to avail himself of it?

The visits of Josiah Redlynch were generally made at night, and Jack guessed that it was about the hour of ten or eleven.

He thought that would be a favourable time to make a descent into the sewer.

There would be less danger of pursuit.

Redlynch was probably drinking with Dartaszan, or some of his boon companions.

Jack was afraid to quit his hold of the block, for fear that it might swing back into its former position, and he should be unable to discover the spring again.

This would be a great calamity.

Crouching on the ground, he bent over the hole and listened attentively.

The sound of water flowing along in a gentle stream, apparently, was distinctly audible.

Occasionally, a dull splash was heard.

This was made by a rat dropping into the water and swimming across to some convenient place, where his companions were either awaiting him or about to follow.

In such a low and nervous state was Jack, that he imagined he heard dismal groans, shrieks, and eries emanating from the recesses of the drain into which he was about to trust himself.

So overwrought was his mind, and so vivid his imagination, that his hand slipped from the block.

The ponderous mass revolved and fitted into its place with a sudden bang, which struck like a knell to the heart of the captive.

With a frantic eagerness, Jack examined the round but rugged surface.

He could discover no trace of the spring.

His nails were torn by his efforts, and his fingers torn and bleeding.

At length, thoroughly exhausted, he sank upon the ground and fainted away.

When he came to himself, he was cold as ice.

The blood in his veins seemed to have stagnated.

To restore his strength and courage, he sought for his loaf of bread and his pitcher of water.

Having found these, he ate and drank heartily, though he at first did so with difficulty.

Poor as this meal was, it not only strengthened and refresheshed him, but gave him a renewed desire for life.

"Oh!" he cried, clasping his hands together, "if I could but escape and cover Fannie with confusion, I should be amply revenged for all that I have suffered in this dismal vault."

Again he attacked the block, feeling every projecting edge or corner with the utmost diligence.

His hand touches something.

It gives.

The block slowly revolves.

The cold air rushes up as before.

The fetid effluvium is again apparent, and Jack knows that he has at length touched the spring for a second time.

With the utmost care, he lowered himself into the aperture, having taken the precaution of propping the block back by means of his pitcher of water.

It could not now swing back and crush his fingers before he allowed himself to drop into the water.

He hesitated before taking the final plunge.

How far had he to drop?

What was the depth of the water?

He might break his legs in falling.

Here was a new danger.

It was no time for delay, however.

Summoning all his courage to his aid, he breathed a fervent prayer to Heaven for aid, and suffered himself to fall.

After dropping about ten or a dozen feet, he came in contact with about three feet of water.

Standing still for a minute, he drew his breath, and wiped away the water which had splashed into his eyes.

The tide flowed, as well as he could discover, to the right of him.

This, then, in all probability, was the road to the lake.

Should he pursue his course, or turn round and endeavour to gain some outlet in a more central position.

He argued that if he reached the lake his progress might be barred by the grating.

So, turning round, he waded slowly through the stream, and went, he knew not whither.

About an hour after this, Josiah Redlynch, who was smoking and drinking in the company of Dartazzan, exclaimed :—

"Something's happened!"

"Something is always happening," returned Dartazzan, philosophically.

"It's serious. I can't tell what it is, but I never see a red hand float in the air before me

but I know some dreadful bad luck is going to happen."

"Bah!" said Dartazzan.

"Laugh as much as you like!" exclaimed Redlynch. "The red hand is in the air. There! there!"

Dartazzan looked in the direction indicated, but could see nothing.

"Of course you can see nothing," said Redlynch; "it's an omen intended for me only."

"A man's superstitions should be respected, and I will not laugh at yours," observed Dartazzan, more gravely.

"Nothing could come into the dungeon," said Redlynch, as if to himself.

"If you think there is the slightest possibility of anything having happened to the prisoner, by all means let us take a light and satisfy ourselves that the bird is safe."

Lighting a candle and taking the key from his pocket, Josiah Redlynch replied :—

"Come on ; it's best to be sure."

The two men descended the stairs which led to the dungeon, and opened the door.

Redlynch, holding the candle high above his head, cried hoarsely—

"Look! He's gone, and through the trap, too. Who was right? Did the red hand come to me for nothing?"

"Extraordinary!" replied Dartazzan, turning rather pale. "What's to be done?"

"Done! Why, one of us must go after him, and hunt him down like a rat. He must never come out alive."

A ferocious expression crossed Redlynch's repulsive features, and he toyed restlessly with a murderous-looking knife which was stuck in his belt.

"One of us!" observed Dartazzan.

"I said so."

"And why not you, my friend?"

"It doesn't follow that because I have always done the dirty work of the firm that I always shall do it. This is a crisis. Our lives depend upon our energy. Come, we will draw lots"

Dartazzan inclined his head in token of assent.

Redlynch took an envelope from his pocket, and tore it in two unequal pieces.

These he put in his hand, and extended it to Dartazzan, who drew one.

It was the longest.

"The choice is mine," exclaimed Dartazzan, "and I leave the job to you."

Uttering a curse, Redlynch at once proceeded to lower himself into the hole as Jack had done.

"Stop!" cried Dartazzan. "Take with you a lantern and a bottle of spirits You will require them both."

Redlynch drew his Herculean frame again on a level with the floor, rose up further, and then sat down on the edge of the hole.

Dartazzan went away, and presently returned with a lantern, and matches, and a bottle of brandy.

These he had tied to a piece of string.

"Drop below," he said, "and I will lower them to you."

"Right," answered Redlynch.

"Give a good account of him."

"If I do not, he shall of me. One of us will die in the drain," answered Redlynch, determinedly.

There was a splash.

The man had dropped into the water.

"Lower away!" he cried, and the order was brought in a sepulchral tone to the vault.

Dartazzan, however, understood what was

meant, and let down the brandy and the lantern.

Redlynch clutched hold of them, and holding the lantern before him, struck off in the direction taken by Jack.

CHAPTER X.

THE FIGHT IN THE DARK.

DESPERATE indeed was the task which Jack had assigned himself.

To wade through the slush and toil on, on in the pitchy darkness until kind Heaven should vouchsafe him some means of exit from the foul and pestilential atmosphere in which he was wandering.

While there is life there is hope.

Never before had Jack so thoroughly appreciated this glorious maxim.

On he pushed, now staggering forward, and falling either into the water or striking himself against the slimy walls of the creek.

How much further would he have to go?

How much longer would his strength enable him to hold out?

These were questions which he asked himself continually.

His long captivity, and the bad fare upon which he had subsisted, had considerably reduced his strength.

Now, an energy born of frantic despair seemed to possess him, and he felt that he was capable of performing wonders.

After tramping along for some time, he came to a higher elevation, where the ground was comparatively dry, only a stream of half a foot in depth winding slowly along.

This was a great relief to him, for his limbs were already beginning to ache from the severity of the exercise he had been taking.

Leaning against the side, he rested a while.

A few rats dashed past him, their bright eyes scintillating like diamonds in the darkness.

The sullen splash they made as they descended into the deeper drain, told him that they were thoroughly familiar with the locality.

And then a horrible thought took possession of his terror-laden mind.

Suppose he were condemned to wander until, his strength exhausted, his frame enfeebled, his courage gone, he fell an easy prey to an army of these same rats, who, while the breath was yet in him, might tear the hot and quivering flesh from his tortured body?

This terrifying reflection, joined to the oppressive sensation brought on by the black and murky darkness, took such a hold upon his his mind that he lifted up his voice and shrieked wildly.

An unearthly echo alone replied to him.

His hair bristled and stood on end, his knees shook together, and he felt for the time being, incapable of any further action.

Fantastic fancies attacked him.

He imagined that he was mocked with demoniacal laughter, and that fiery monsters continually passed and repassed him.

It was some time before he could recover from the state of panic into which he had been thrown.

But recognising the necessity for action, and becoming convinced of the folly of his supernatural conceptions, he bethought him how he should proceed.

Hitherto, he had been looking down.

Now he resolved to look up, so that he might see any opening above, or any grating which com-

Just as he was on the point of starting, he glanced in the direction from whence he had come, and beheld a flickering light like a star in the distance.

What could it be?

Was it one of the assassins from whom he had just escaped, close upon his footsteps, following him up with a persistence which, in its savage energy and unrelenting determination, meant death?

The thought inspired him with a new terror.

If it were so, small indeed was his chance of escape!

Unarmed, lacking physical strength, weary with the exertions he had already undergone, he feared that he would fall an easy prey to the assassin.

Should he fly?

This he could not resolve to do.

And for this reason:

He argued that it was extremely improbable that either Josiah Redlynch or the more astute villain Dartazzan, were yet upon his track, or, indeed, had discovered his escape.

The chances were very much in favour of the advancing man being friend instead of foe.

So Jack stood his ground.

As the stranger came gradually nearer and nearer, wading laboriously through the water, his anxiety became intense.

His heart beat wildly against his breast.

He could scarcely draw his breath.

Life, liberty—all depended upon the identity of, and the attitude displayed by, the stranger!

The lantern shed its ruddy glare around, and enabled Jack's unaccustomed eyes, half-dazzled as they were, to decipher the hateful features of an enemy.

An enemy sworn and determined.

The stranger was Josiah Redlynch.

Nerving himself with an energy which despair alone could give, Jack darted forward, resolving to take the initiative.

He had perceived that Josiah Redlynch carried in his right hand the lantern, in his left a murderous-looking knife, while a dagger was stuck carelessly in a leather belt, which went around his waist.

Redlynch did not perceive his antagonist until he was upon him.

With a rapid movement Jack seized the dagger, and with the other hand he dashed the lantern from the ruffian's grasp, sending it flying some distance through the air.

It fell into the water, which speedily extinguished it.

Sudden as all this was, the light was not put out before Josiah Redlynch had recognised his antagonist.

He made a lunge with his knife in the direction in which he supposed him to be standing.

But Jack had foreseen this.

As soon as he had accomplished the enterprise he had so rapidly conceived, and as easily executed, he stepped back some paces.

Then each one listened for the breathing of the other, as it is by that means alone that they could tell the position of the enemy.

Jack began to gain courage.

He had secured a weapon with which to fight, and he had placed his opponent at a disadvantage. These were things to be well considered, and thought highly of.

Redlynch now blamed the hasty and imprudent manner in which he had advanced.

To this also he owed the terror with which he

Nevertheless, he held Jack for a contemptible antagonist, and had no doubt whatever that he should eventually succeed in slaying him.

He had sworn to do so.

It was with that express intention that he had descended into the sewer.

His safety and that of his friend Dartazzan depended on Jack's death.

That alone could save them.

He would not have cared much about his companion in crime, Dartazzan's safety, but they were so mixed up together and identified, that if one fell, it was probable the other would fall also.

A heavy breathing close by him warned Jack of approaching danger.

With a spring he retreated a few paces.

It was lucky he did so.

The harsh grating of a knife against the wall became distinctly audible, and a deep curse, uttered by Redlynch, warned him of the proximity of the villain.

This was Jack's opportunity.

He did not neglect it.

Dashing forward, so as to make sure of his prey, he aimed a desperate blow at the place in which he supposed him to be standing.

His dagger encountered some resistance.

Drawing it back, he again retreated, to avoid similar treatment.

As he did so, his ears were regaled by the sound of a loud cry, as of someone in pain.

He could not doubt that he had wounded Redlynch severely.

If so, the advantage at the commencement of the combat was with him.

He fervently prayed God that he might retain it.

The dagger had wounded Redlynch in the left shoulder, causing an effusion of blood, but not entirely disabling the arm.

Redlynch thought that he was wrong to permit this fighting in the dark, so he felt in his pocket for some matches, and retired up the drain until he kicked something with his foot which he supposed to be his lantern.

He was right in his conjecture.

Striking a match upon a rough button of his coat, he picked up the lantern, squeezed the wick of the candle dry with his fingers, and succeeded in lighting it once more.

During this operation he kept his eye fixed intently upon Jack, who, with a weakness wholly inexcusable, feared to rush forward and attack him.

He should have frustrated this effort at all hazards.

But he did not do so.

The consequence of this supine folly soon became apparent.

Josiah Redlynch calmly bound up his wound with his neckerchief.

Then, with the lantern to guide his footsteps, and his knife uplifted, he advanced towards Jack, who, once again half panic-stricken, was crouching against the wall.

At length he retreated, being aroused to a consciousness of the danger of his position.

Redlynch quickened his pace.

Jack kept in front until he came to a spot where the water deepened.

Here he halted.

Josiah Redlynch took advantage of his temporary hesitation.

With a yell like that of a wild beast, he sprang upon him.

The lantern fell to the ground as before, and the two were soon grappling in the darkness,

desperate results involved in the contest could have inspired.

CHAPTER XI.

JACK'S STERN SENSE OF JUSTICE.

THE battle did not continue long.

Luck was on Jack's side.

Redlynch slipped just as he was about to plunge his knife into Harkaway's side, and the latter, hurling himself upon him, drove the dagger with which he was armed straight for the ruffian's heart.

He hit his mark.

With a low moan the fellow sank into the water, and never moved more.

That was the end of him.

Jack breathed a heart-felt prayer of gratitude to the Almighty, for he felt that he had escaped a great danger—one of the greatest, perhaps, that had ever beset him in the course of an adventurous career.

For a while he leaned against the side of the creek to recover from the nervous excitement into which this event had thrown him.

The strongest man gives way sometimes.

Jack was no exception to this rule.

But his hesitation was only momentary.

Recovering himself, he dived in the water for the body, and to make sure of having rid the earth of a villain who richly deserved death, he plunged his dagger once more into him.

Satisfied that Redlynch was dead, he now began to think how he could get out of the creek.

Its waters had chilled him to the bone, and it was with difficulty that he waded through them.

More by luck than design, he, after wandering about half a mile, saw a glimmering of light in the distance.

He had come to the end of the boarding over of the creek.

This is to say, he had reached the limits of the town, and was free to follow the watercourse to the lake in which it made an outlet, and this was not far off.

The channel contracted itself a little at the opening, and he had to crawl on his hands and knees to get out.

But this was nothing.

Wet and chilled, he reached the open air, and saw the starry sky overhead and breathed the atmosphere of liberty once more.

"Thank Heaven!" he exclaimed.

Climbing up the bank, he looked inland, and the lights of Flyaway Gap showed him he was not far distant from the miners' settlement.

"First Dartazzan," he muttered, "and then Fannie."

His face wore a stern and grave expression, which boded no good to either of the persons he had mentioned.

Shaking the water off his clothes as well as he was able, he walked to the Gap, and went into the saloon which we have had occasion to speak of as the "Little Brown Jug."

He was so cold, and felt so weak, that he wanted some brandy, and as this was the first saloon he came to, he thought he would enter it, not knowing that it was the resort of rowdies, and that it had been the favourite haunt of Spanish Joe, Gosh, Redlynch, and the other desperadoes of the Gap.

It may be readily imagined that Jack presented a miserable appearance after his captivity and his immersion in the water.

He was dirty, mud-begrimed, and disrepu-

But in spite of his beggarly aspect, there was a look in his face, and something in his way of carrying himself, that showed he was not what his clothes and appearance would lead a casual observer to suppose.

The "Little Brown Jug" was crowded with the inmates of the "Crow's Nest," who were playing dominoes, euchre, and seven-up for drinks, which were repeated with alarming frequency.

Going up to the bar, Jack, who was shivering with cold, exclaimed to the bar-tender—

"Will you give me a drink of brandy without the money?"

"No hang-up here," replied the man.

"I'm able to pay."

"Who are you?"

"Jack Harkaway. I live up in the woods, and will send you the money in the morning. I've been robbed and roughly treated."

"Is that so?"

The man looked doubtingly at him.

He had half a mind to trust him, and yet he did not like to, as he was not one of his regular customers, and had had considerable experience of dead beats.

Jack had spoken loudly, for he did not care what opinion the crowd formed of him.

One man, who was sitting at a table near by, got up and was going towards the door.

"Hold on there, sir," said the bar-tender. "You haven't settled."

"Let it wait," was the reply.

"It's against the boss's orders."

"Oh! to —— with your boss," answered the man.

The bar-tender drew a revolver from the pistol-pocket of his pants, and came out into the room.

"Now, see here," he cried, "this ain't good enough for me."

"What do you mean?"

"What I say. Look-a-here, Dartazzan, if you try to play points on me, I'll lay you out."

"You will, will you?"

"Yes, sir. I've kept bar in rougher places than this, and I never let anyone get the best of me yet. Plank down."

"To-morrow, I tell you."

"That's too thin. I've heard you say that you pulled off a stake——"

"Was going to," interrupted the customer.

"No matter; you've been talking about this great stake ever so long."

"But I haven't scooped in the stamps yet. Good-night."

"Look-a-here! That won't do. Pay up, or——"

"Wipe down your chin."

The bar-tender restlessly moved the pistol, and, with a sudden movement, Jack seized it.

"What did you do that for?" cried the bar-tender.

"I know that man," replied Harkaway.

"You do?"

"Yes. I have just killed his friend, Redlynch, and I'm going to kill him. Stand on one side."

He cocked the pistol.

The bar-tender did not know what to do, and stood irresolute.

No sooner had Jack heard him mention the name of Dartazzan than he turned round.

He recognised his enemy, who was the hired assassin of Mrs. Cabuchon.

His sense of justice was a stern one.

Without giving Dartazzan any time to draw a bead on him, he fired at his head.

The pistol carried true.

Dartazzan fell, with a bullet through his skull, and was stretched on the floor in the cold embrace of death.

All the rowdies in the room were up in a moment.

Their cards and drinks were deserted.

Every one of them knew Dartazzan, and they were only too ready to revenge his death.

They thought it was a cowardly and drunken shot.

A dozen pistols were levelled at Jack.

He did not flinch.

Cold, hungry, and weak as he was, by reason of the trials he had gone through, he faced the mob.

Extending his hand, he cried—

"Shoot if you want to, but let me get in a word first."

"What have you to say?" inquired a man over six feet high, who was known among his associates as Coyote Joe.

"Not much; but what I do say will be to the point."

"Hurry up."

"This man tried to have me killed. He was hired to do it along with Redlynch, but I got the best of them on that deal; and if you want to shoot me for just giving a man as good as he sent, I'm standing right here—mind that! I'm not running, and though I have more than one life left in my pistol, to show you that I am no bar-room rowdy, I will throw it away."

Jack threw the pistol on the floor.

"Now then," he said, "you have heard my explanation; if you want to kill an unarmed man, you are at liberty to do it, though that is not United States custom, as a rule.

"Who are you, anyway?" inquired Coyote Joe.

"Jack Harkaway."

"Him's as living up in the woods with a lot of Sioux Indians?"

"Yes."

"Come here in search of the Mountain of Gold?"

"Yes," said Jack, again.

Coyote Joe turned to some of his friends, and conversed with them in a low tone.

"Then," he exclaimed, addressing Jack once more, " me and my mates don't want to act roughly; but we knew Dartazzan and Redl nch. You own to wiping the pair out, and you say in justification that they tried to kill you."

"That's true," said Jack.

"We've only your word for that."

"Isn't that good enough?"

"Not in a case like this," exclaimed Coyote Joe; "we don't know you. If you was one of us, we could reckon you up, and just say right away how you'd pan out, but it's different; here's a man who's one of the gang shot down right before our noses, and we've got to have satisfaction, and don't you forget it, unless we see that he deserved it. Dart was a contrary cuss, I'll allow that, and not at all particular as to how he got the stamps to pay for his rum. That don't make a darned bit of difference. I suppose none of us are angels, and we can't none of us show a clear record.

"Well," said Jack, "you have made quite a little speech What is the upshot of it?"

"Just this, squire: Can you prove what you say?"

"Prove what?"

"That Josh Redlynch and Dart had it in for you?"

"Why, certainly I can."

"By whom?"

"Member of his own family."

"Whose? Redlynch's?"

"Yes."

"I'll bet that Sally wouldn't go back on her old man," said Coyote Joe, with a knowing wink. "I have known her some time, and she's got grit in her. If she an't, I want to see the next."

"I am not talking of her. It is of Lily Redlynch that I speak. She is a good and pure girl as far as I know, and I feel positive that she will tell you I had ample cause to kill her father and this fellow here, whom you call Dartazzan."

"Very well. We'll send for her," replied Coyote Joe.

"Yes, yes," shouted the miners. "Let Lily Redlynch settle this case. Stand over him, Joe, with your iron cocked, while a few of the boys goes and fetches Lily."

"I'm right here, boys," said Coyote Joe.

Half a dozen men started off for Redlynch's house, to bring Lily back to the saloon.

She was to prove the truth or falsehood of Jack's statement.

The result of their journey meant one of two things.

Life or death.

It was a trying moment for Harkaway, but he saw that his bold speech had produced a good effect upon these rough and lawless men, who would have shot him down like a dog if they had felt like it.

But there was a sense of even-handed justice about them.

In their own language, they were "willing to give a fellow a chance."

Out there in Flyaway Gap Jack could have been murdered and thrown out in a back-yard, without anyone taking the trouble to dig a hole to bury him.

If the boys heard that he had killed Redlynch and shot Dartazzan, the verdict would have been, "Served him right."

As for Dartazzan, his dead body remained on the floor where it had fallen.

No one took the trouble to cover it up, or close the staring, wide-open eyes, which were rapidly glazing.

A pool of blood had collected on the boards, and a tiny stream ran down towards the door.

Men came up to the bar with bloody boots, for they stepped and splashed in it, as if it had been water.

"Come, boys," said one man. "Step up lively. It's a long time between drinks."

Five men walked up to the bar, preceded by the man who had invited them.

"Set 'em up agin," continued the man. "I am good for it."

The barman did not move a glass.

"What's the matter with you?" said the man.

"See here, Comstock," said the barman, "the slate's full."

The man was called Comstock from having been a master in the Comstock Lode Mine, Virginia City, Nevada.

"The deuce it is!" said Comstock. "Can't you hang it up?"

"No, sir. Wait till the master comes in."

"The master be hanged! Set 'em up, I say! It's no use a-talkin', you've got to do it, you!"

"Can't be done! The slate's full."

"Guess I'll have to manage this bar till the master comes in!" said Comstock.

He deliberately drew his pistol and took aim at the barman.

The latter put his hand behind him, as if to produce his weapon, but Comstock was too quick for him.

He fired.

The barman fell.

"It's no use a-kickin', boys, 'gainst this gang. We're Modocs," said Comstock, quickly.

"Good for you, Com!" replied the "boys."

"Run him out, and lay him alongside Dart. If I ain't mistaken, there'll be a few more laid out before the night's over."

The body of the barman was placed by the side of Dartazzan.

He was not quite dead, but no one took any notice of him.

Comstock went behind the counter, and placed a whisky-bottle before his friends.

"Sail in bald-headed!" he exclaimed. "Take a bumper each of you. There's more where that came from, and it's cheap at that."

Harkaway had looked on in horror at the scene of violence.

"Come, stranger," continued Comstock. "This bear I laid out wouldn't trust you for a drink, but I will. You're just likely's not to be shot in five minutes, so you'd best line yourself. There's no objection to that, is there, Coyote?"

"Not a durned bit!" replied Coyote Joe, who stood over Jack with a pistol. "If the cap ain't too high-toned to drink with us fellows, he's welcome to all the poison he can get out of this shanty."

"I'll take some brandy," replied Jack, who really stood in need of something.

"That's only coloured alcohol," said Comstock."

"We ain't got no fancy drinks at the Gap. Take your bourbon or your whisky, and look pleasant."

Jack did as he was advised, and felt that the spirit, bad as it was, put new life into him.

Scarcely had he set down the glass than Lily Redlynch entered with the men who had been sent for her.

They had found her home.

She knew nothing about what had happened.

Coyote Joe stood close by Jack, prepared to shoot him at a moment's notice.

Comstock had more delicacy than the rest, and he took off his coat and threw it over the faces of the dead men.

But Lily's eye was too quick.

"Dartazzan!" she exclaimed. "Is he dead, and Charley?"

This was the name of the unfortunate barman.

"Been a little mess, miss," said Comstock, by way of explanation.

She looked around her timidly.

Most of the men in the crowd were known to her, and she had frequently come in contact with Charley, the barman, having been sent by her parents for drink to the "Brown Jug."

Her eyes fell upon Jack.

"Mr. Harkaway!" she exclaimed, in surprise.

"You know me, Lily," he exclaimed, "and you thought I was dead, perhaps, and——"

Coyote Joe interfered.

"Stop your tongue," he exclaimed; "we don't want you to put words in the gal's mouth."

"All right," answered Jack.

"What do you want with me?" said Lily.

"These men told me that I was required at the 'Jug,' and I came."

"Do you know this man?" asked Coyote Joe.

"Which one?"

"Harkaway."

"Yes, I do."

"What do you know of him?"

How Jack prayed at that moment that she would speak the truth!

The girl, however, hesitated.

"Are you a vigilance committee?" she inquired.

"Not a darned bit."

"You mean no harm to father?"

"No."

"Then I will tell you. Harkaway was a prisoner in our house, and I gave him his food. Father had to kill him, because a lady paid him to do it, and I thought he was dead; but say, some of you, where's father? Mother's been waiting supper for him ever so long."

Coyote Joe looked at Jack.

"You can go," he said. "But hold on one moment. Miss Lily!"

"Yes, sir," she exclaimed.

"Was Dartazzan in this thing?"

"He brought Mr. Harkaway to father's. It was he who planned it all."

"Good enough. Clear out, Harkaway," said Coyote Joe, "and you can have another drink if you like. I'm not feeling like giving you a bullet, because I like Dartazzan; but there's nothing mean about me, and as Comstock has taken this bar, liquor's cheap to-night."

"No more, thank you all the same," replied Jack.

"Well, I'll drink instead. Here's wishing we may all live long," answered Joe.

Lily looked at Comstock.

"Where's father?" she asked.

Comstock was rapidly becoming intoxicated. Not thinking of the consequences of blurting out the truth, he replied—

"Harkaway cut him, and he's dead."

"Dead! Father dead!"

"He says so."

"And were you going to shoot him if I hadn't come down here?"

"Yes."

The girl's eyes flashed fire.

"Have I saved him?"

"You have that."

"And he killed my father?"

"That's what they say, my girl."

Lily turned very pale.

Then she reeled and fell down in a faint, rolling over the bodies of Charley and Dartazzan.

"She's dead," said one.

"Not she," replied another. "It's only a woman's faint. Let her alone. She'll come to. If she don't, what the deuce odds is it? Pass the drinks, Comstock, and hand us the grog; we'll finish our game of Casino."

Jack took one glance of a pitying nature at Lily, and quitted the saloon.

He knew that she was in no danger, and that his staying there could possibly do her no good.

It would have been folly to remain in such a hard crowd, as his life would not have been safe amongst them.

It was growing late, and he hurried home.

In an hour he reached the settlement.

There were lights in Hank's dwelling, and Jack paused a moment outside the door of the rude log-hut.

He distinguished the voices of Hank and Monday.

"See here, Mas' Hank!" exclaimed Monday. "Um got to go after Harkaway somewhere."

"That's true enough," replied Hank; "but what direction air we ter start fur?"

"Hunston's got him again, sure."

"Well, it may be so, and we'll explore this island to-morrow. Ef the cap's on it we'll find him, yer kin bet yer sweet life on it."

"Now um talk like um man. Massa Jack and I been together many years, and I not like to see um lost like this."

Jack pressed the latch of the door and entered.

A kerosene-lamp was burning on the table, and both men were smoking their pipes over a bottle of whisky.

"I have heard your remarks!" exclaimed Jack, "and am glad to save you the trouble of your intended excursion."

Hank seized Harkaway by the hand.

"Welcome home, kernel," he said. "I didn't think they'd shoot yer."

The other hand was grasped by Monday.

"By thunder, Massa Jack!" he cried, "this is better than a house and lot to me. Hooray! Come back safe, after all!"

"Yes; and I've had another close shave of it."

"Had um squeak, eh?"

"I have that," said Jack.

"Lick um dead-beat Hunston again?"

"It wasn't Hunston this time."

"Who then?"

Jack closed the door.

"Where's Harvey?" he asked.

"Mist' Harvey gone to bed, I guess, sar."

"Go and rouse him up."

"Want um here?"

"Yes, right away; but tell him to ask Hilda not to say a word."

"That all right, sah. Goily! how good um feel!" replied Monday.

"Hold on," said Hank. "If there's anything secret that the Kernal wants ter say, best bring Mrs. Harvey along."

"Why?" asked Jack.

"Because women can't keep a secret, especially if they only know half of it."

"How?"

"You don't want that fraud, Mrs. Cabuchon —late Ghost-in-the-Wood—to know anything?"

"Right," said Jack. "Hank's advice is good. Go and bring Harvey and his wife here, but tell them Hank requires their presence."

Monday nodded and went off.

"Cap, you look bad," said Hank.

"So would you, if you had gone through what I have," said Jack.

"Been hard used?"

"Just hear it all, and you'll say so. It was only by God's mercy that I escaped."

"I'll wait till Mr. and Mrs. Harvey come, and it'll save yer two tellings."

"That's so."

A few minutes elapsed.

Then Dick and Hilda entered the hut.

Their surprise was as great as their delight, which was unbounded.

"Why, Jack, dear old boy!" exclaimed Harvey, "you are like a ghost from the grave."

"Give me up this time, eh?" said Jack, with a hard smile.

"We had, indeed."

"And you, Hilda?"

"*Mazzal tob*," cried Hilda. "That is our Hebrew way of wishing you good luck, you know. *Mazzal tob*, Jack, as long as you live."

But turning her gaze in the direction of the south-east, the saw a boat turning the bend.

In it was a man.

The recognition was mutual.

"Mr. Hunston!" said Fannie.

"Why, Mrs Cabuchon!" replied the occupant of the boat, who was no other than Hunston, "what on earth are you doing here, at this time of the morning?"

CHAPTER XII.

THE TREASURE.

"I MIGHT ask you the same question," she answered.

Her spirits began to revive at meeting a former friend of her husband, and a well-known hater of Jack Harkaway.

If she was bound by her promise, and could not strike herself, she could strike through somebody else.

She would live.

She would make friends with Hunston.

It should be his hand that struck the blow, but hers should be the one that guided his.

"I can easily explain my presence here," he replied.

"Aren't you afraid of Harkaway?" she asked, her voice trembling a little as she pronounced the name.

"I? You never saw me weaken yet at the sight of a man."

"Indeed!"

"No, not the best man that was ever born."

"Do you hate him as much as ever?"

"More."

"We have not met," said Fannie, "since the day I saved him from you. And I am sorry I did it, now!"

"You were Ghost-that-Lies-in-the-Wood then," replied Hunston. "Now you are the Blonde Beauty again. You settled Cabuchon. Well perhaps you were right."

"Shall not a woman avenge her wrongs?"

"Why, certainly. Cabuchon behaved badly to you, as I know, and you were justified in doing what you did."

"I have tried my hardest to return Mr. Harkaway's treatment," said Fannie, "but I've failed."

"So have I in the same line, though I did my level best in that direction."

"Don't you think Harkaway deserves my anger?"

"Now, you've got advantage of me," returned Hunston. "I don't know what has happened, but I know he doesn't like you, for I hear him say once that he would sooner marry the devil's daughter and live with the old folks than make you his wife."

A look of bitter enmity crossed Fannie's face.

"Is that so?"

What Hunston had said was infamously untrue, but he had a motive in saying it.

"His wife is dead," continued Fannie, musingly. "She was his second wife, too; and I don't know that I am homely."

"You are charming."

"Do you think so?" she asked with a smile.

"But you have made a mistake in one thing," continued Hunston.

"What is that?"

"Jack's wife lives!"

"Really! Is Viola alive?"

"Yes."

"And the boy?"

"Both of them. Mrs. Harkaway and Young Jack have the honour to be my prisoners."

"Yours?"

Fannie clapped her hands together with delight.

"Oh! Mr. Hunston," she exclaimed, "can we not form a bond of union, and let our object be to crush this proud man who tramples on our feelings, and seems to think the world was made for him?"

"Harkaway, do you mean?"

"Who else?"

"Of course we can; but first tell me what brought you here this morning, and what has happened in the camp?"

Fannie related to him what had occurred, and he listened attentively to every word which fell from her lips.

"By George!" he cried. "You came very near finishing him. We can't always make sure of these things. He killed Redlynch and Dartazzan just as he did Spanish Joe and Gosh. Bad luck for us. Very."

"You say 'us.'"

"Yes. We will work together, and you shall think no more of committing suicide."

"I am so lonely and friendless and hopeless, now," she answered, with a sigh, casting down her eyes.

"You shall be no longer so."

"How?"

She was blushing up to the temples now, and, her formerly pale face became red as fire.

Did she guess what he was about to say?

"If I might only say what I have in my mind. Shall I offend you? May I?—dare I?" he began.

"Speak freely," she said. "I am a woman of the world, Mr. Hunston."

"If you give me permission, I will. Beautiful Fannie, I love you. I will marry you, if you will have me; only say the word."

She boldly placed her hand in his.

"I am yours," she said.

Hunston was overjoyed.

Strange and sudden as his proposition was, he was in earnest.

He had long been an admirer in secret of Mrs. Cabuchon, and her adventurous disposition, fierce longing for revenge, and undying hatred when anyone offended her, were strong passports to his favour.

"It is a bargain," he said. "When shall we be married?"

"At once."

"How?"

"There is a priest at the Gap," she replied, with a bitter smile. "He was to have married me to Jack Harkaway."

"Was to?"

"Yes. Do you not remember what I told you? When Dartazzan and Redlynch had made him prisoner, I offered to spare his life if he would have me for a wife."

"Unfeeling wretch!" said Hunston.

"We will make him suffer. Will we not, dear?"

"Indeed, we will, and through those he holds most dear."

"Oh, yes. That is a splendid idea. When you take me with you as your bride to your camp, I may have Viola and Young Jack as my slaves?"

"Certainly."

"May I beat them, and treat them like negroes in Cuba, if they displease me?"

"Lick them within an inch of their lives, my darling. Kill them, if you wish," said Hunston.

"Oh, that will be grand!" cried Fannie, clapping her hands.

Huston approached Fannie, and encircled her waist with his arm

"One kiss?" he said, tenderly.

He was a good-looking young fellow, and the loss of an eye did not detract much from his personal appearance.

Fannie thought he was very manly and handsome, but she turned away bashfully, with the coquetry natural to a woman

"Oh, that won't do. You are mine now," he continued.

She let him kiss her after a little struggle.

"This is the happiest day of my life," said Hunston. "Do you love money, Fannie?"

Hers was one of the mercenary natures which are very fond of money, because it supplies people with all sorts of luxuries.

"Yes," she said ; "but do not let that trouble you. I know you are poor. We shall be happy together in the wilderness. Here we want very little, and money would be useless to us."

"That is true. Yet I do not propose to live all my life in these hills."

"I should be contented if I had you all the time."

"Would you not like to shine in good society —be a star on the Continent, dazzle in London and Paris, and taste all the joys of life in the great centres of civilisation?"

"Yes."

"You shall do it."

"How?"

"Listen!" he exclaimed. "I was sailing home——"

"In your boat?" she asked.

"It is not mine. I had a fight for it. I stole it. The boat belonged to a man named Hurston, a miner, and he sailed after me. I shot him."

"Is he dead?"

"Yes, and at the bottom of the lake, for I tied a rock to his neck and let him sink."

"I love you, dear!" exclaimed Fannie, "Because you do not trifle with your enemies. We are very much alike."

"When I had slain Hurston," continued Huston. "I was going to Olalla's camp——"

"Is Olalla with you?" she interrupted.

"He is."

"And all his men?"

"Oh, no! The Crows and Bannocks are nearly all dead. He has but two Indians."

"And your camp consists of——"

"Viola, Young Jack, Olalla and two Indians, and a negro named Pete."

"Oh, yes, I remember. Lord Mossbunker's negro. I carried him off to wait on Viola and Young Jack when I put them in the cave. How did they escape?"

Hunston hurriedly told her all he knew about that, and his adventures after his escape from Ate-we-an-pe, until he settled at the hut of Old Swamp, on the island in the lake.

"Go on," she answered. "I am much obliged to you for the information, and sorry for interrupting you."

"Well," said Hunston, "it appears that this fellow I killed was a miser. He had a claim, on which he found a lot of money. He was afraid someone would murder and rob him, so he buried his gold on his lot His suspicions were so far correct that some ruffian did come one night and burn his house over his head, but his gold was buried in the earth in bags, and they got nothing This so alarmed Hurston that he sold his lot to a man named Tom Wanzer, and Hurston has lately been waiting for an opportunity to dig up his gold and get away from the Gap."

"How do you know this?"

"When I shot the old boy I rifled his pockets, and found a pocketbook, in which he kept a diary, and from successive entries I got all this information."

"Do you think it reliable?"

"I do."

"Did you know Wanzer or Hurston?"

"I am not acquainted with anyone at the Gap, but I intend to go to Tom Wanzer and ask permission to look over this old claim of Hurston's."

"Will he grant it?"

"No doubt. He thinks it worthless."

"And then——"

"Well, after that," said Hunston, "I will dig up the gold, bring it to the boat, and take the treasure with us to Olalla."

"That is good."

"As soon as we have settled our scores with Harkaway, we can go the East again and be big guns."

"That will be nice," said Fannie.

All her woman's vanity was aroused, for she found Hunston a man after her own heart, and felt that she had something to live for.

"First of all," continued Hunston, "we will draw this boat up on the beach."

"Yes."

"Then we will go and get married by your priest."

"I do not wish for any delay. My hand and heart are yours," answered Fannie.

"Then," said Hunston, "you shall return along the beach to the boat. In the locker aft, I have provisions and fresh water. You will eat and wait for me. As soon as I have secured the treasure which the miser buried I will return to you."

"Have you directions to find it?"

"Oh! yes. He says in his diary, 'Go to my burnt hut. Face the window on the ground floor, looking east. Then take twelve paces. After which turn to the right and take six paces. Dig down. You will find a box which is empty. Under that is a slab of stone, and beneath that are a quantity of bags filled with nuggets and gold-dust.'"

"What made him write that?"

"I cannot tell. If he died, I guess he did not want his secret to perish with him."

"Anyhow, you are in luck," said Fannie.

"I am," said Hunston, with a gleam of perfect satisfaction.

This singular meeting, which resulted in a still more singular marriage, showed what strange things happen in this world.

Neither Fannie nor Hunston expected anything of the kind when day broke.

One was going in search of a treasure, and the other was hovering over the brink of the grave.

They beached the boat and walked to the Gap, where they experienced no difficulty in finding the man who had been an ordained minister in Massachusetts, before he ran away to the Black Hills to escape the consequences of some irregularity of conduct.

He was playing cards in the Crow's Nest, and when told what his services were required for, he stated the amount of his fee, received it, and married Hunston to Fannie Cabuchon, the Blonde Beauty, in the back parlour of the saloon.

Could a marriage made under such circumstances result in happiness?

It was extremely doubtful whether it would, but there was one sympathetic cord between them, one bond of union, as Fannie had phrased it, which could not be severed, and that was their mutual hatred for Jack Harkaway.

When the ceremony, if it can be dignified with that name, was over, Hunston walked with his bride to the limits of Flyaway Gap, and directed her to proceed to the boat.

"No one will interfere with you," he said, "as old Hurston, the late owner, is dead. I will join you as soon as I have unearthed the treasure."

"How long do you suppose it will take you?" she asked.

"Oh! maybe five or six hours, perhaps more."

"What a long time to wait!" she exclaimed, pouting her pretty lips.

"Can't be helped, my darling," he exclaimed, "I'll be with you before dark."

"There is a moon, and we can sail away till we find some bay to anchor in. Don't be nervous about me; my head's as level as most people's, and you will never have occasion to call me a fool."

"I'm sure of that," she answered, adding, "well I will wait and watch. May you have all the luck you can wish for."

So the husband kissed the wife, with every demonstration of affection, and thus separated to meet again near the Giant's Rock, where the boat was beached.

Hunston returned to the Gap, and made inquiries for Tom Wanzer, who owned Hurston's lot, which was everywhere regarded as a worked-out claim.

A half-witted boy, named Slinking Sammy, from his shambling gait, showed him where Tom Wanzer lived, in consideration of a bit of silver which Hunston gave him.

Wanzer was a well-to-do miner, who believed in the future of Flyaway Gap; consequently he purchased small parcels of real estate when he could get them.

Every week brought fresh settlers to the Gap, and the output of gold continued to increase.

Hunston found Tom Wanzer smoking a cigar on the step of his house.

"Morning!" he exclaimed. "My name's Hunston, and I want to see you on a little business."

"Sail in, my man!" exclaimed Wanzer.

"You've got a piece of land; it's called the Burnt Hut Field, I believe; I want to look over it with a view to purchase."

"That's good," said Wanzer.

"It's worked out, and I guess is'nt worth much."

"Make me an offer and we'll talk; the former owner was said to have got dust out of it, but no one ever knew what he did with his findings."

"I'm just going to take a stroll through the town, and make a few inquiries," continued Hunston. "I'll be back again soon."

"Amuse yourself all you please, Mr. Hunston," replied Wanzer.

Hunston took his walk, not because he wanted it, but he did not care to be too anxious lest he should arouse the suspicions of Wanzer, who, in that case, would not allow him to go to the land.

Going into a saloon, Hunston once more took out the MS. book, and re-read the instructions respecting the treasure which the dead miner had written.

He reflected over the matter, and went again to Wanzer to ask the way to the disused claim.

Hunston was so extremely anxious to possess the treasure of which he had read in the manuscript that he would not wait until the shades of night fell, and he was so mercenary that he would ask no one's assistance.

If there was a treasure, he would enjoy it himself, and share it with no one.

Thomas Wanzer, as owner of the lot, could, of course, put in a claim for anything found on his property.

He was a man of resources.

He was not an antiquary, but he really had a taste and a fancy for anything old and unquestionably of ancient origin.

Therefore, digging for a treasure just suited him.

He shouldered a spade and a pickaxe, which he borrowed, and told Thomas Wanzer that he was going now to the field, as he had a mind to turn up his ground in a particular spot, in the hopes of finding some gold.

"Go along, Hunston," said Wanzer. "I hope you may find a lot of gold which will lay the foundation of your fortune."

"If I were to come across a treasure——"

"Why, you have my permission to keep it," interrupted Thomas, "for you will have deserved it. A man who takes trouble ought to have something for it. I know one thing, however, and that is, I would not give you a pound for your chance."

"Do you mean to say that there is no gold nor silver in the earth?"

"I will not say that."

"Do I understand that I have your permission to keep anything I can find?"

"Certainly you have," replied the miner, with a laugh, which indicated that he did not believe in anything being found on that claim.

Hunston was not altogether satisfied with this response.

He was sure of finding something, which if his information was correct, would be of considerable value, and he induced Thomas to give him the promise in writing, which he did.

Armed with this precious document, he set out for the ruins of the hut, and repeated to himself the instructions which the manuscript gave him.

The hut was not of great size.

A portion of the walls remained, though they were shockingly dilapidated.

Vines had grown over them, giving them a picturesque appearance.

When he reached the hut, which was surrounded and shut out of view by a number of old funereal-looking trees, he threw down his pick and his spade, and walked to the window, from the centre of which he took twelve paces.

Having accomplished this, he turned to the right and took six paces.

Having made an indentation in the ground with his heel, he picked up his shovel, and taking off his coat and turning up his shirt-sleeves, began work.

Where the earth was hard he used his pickaxe, and after an hour's labour, during which he had made a trench four feet by three, and five deep, he struck something hard.

This, on examination, turned out to be a box made of hickory wood.

It was heavy, and cost him prodigious labour to raise it up.

At length he did raise it, and contrived to stand it on end.

It was entirely out of his power to lift it out of the trench.

Hunston did not leave off, though some time had elapsed.

He was anxious to find the treasure.

Seizing his pickaxe, Hunston, after a brief rest, once more attacked the soil, which was flinty and hard.

"I've been as quick as I could," whimpered Slinking Sammy, who seemed to stand in considerable dread of Hunston since he received the castigation at his hands.

"You've come, that's something in your favour. I thought you might have bolted. Wheel the barrow up here. Look alive!"

When the barrow came near enough, Hunston opened the lid of the hamper, and propped it up with a piece of stick.

Then he stooped down and raised up the bags of gold, and placed them one by one in the receptacle he had provided for them.

It was a large basket, and held its freight well.

It was a pity that he had broken bulk in one case, but he took care not to repeat his error.

He handled the rotten canvas with the greatest care, and packed the bags away with the air of a man who is guarding a pearl beyond all price.

Those lumps which were scattered he picked up and placed at the top, covering them with some rank grass, which prevented them from falling about.

"Can you lift it?" he said to Slinking Sammy.

Sammy seized the handles of the barrow, and pushed it a little way. Then he dropped it saying :—

"Too heavy!"

"Oh, that's all nonsense!" cried Hunston, who felt annoyed beyond measure at the idiot's inability to move the gold.

He tried the weight of it himself, and found that it was in reality too heavy to be carried any distance.

Here was a dilemma.

What was to be done?

While he was ruminating, an asinine hee-haw, ringing through the air close by, saluted his ears.

It at once occurred to him that if he could harness the donkey in some way to the barrow, the difficulty would be solved.

Acting with his usual promptitude upon this idea, he left the hut and caught the donkey, leading it back by its mane.

It was quiet and passive, as most donkeys are, and made no resistance.

Fortunately, he had provided himself with a coil of rope, thinking that it might be wanted in his treasure-seeking operations.

He took off his vest, and with it made a sort of apology for a collar.

If it did nothing else, it prevented the rope from galling the animal's neck and hurting his throat.

At length he fastened the barrow to his satisfaction, and bade the idiot lead the donkey while he walked by the side of the hamper, and took care that it did not fall off.

"Hurrah!" he cried, brimful of glee at the success of his plan. "It will ride beautifully like that."

Slinking Sammy had since his thrashing been silent and sulky.

If Hunston had not been so elated at the idea of possessing so much gold, he would not have failed to notice that the so-called idiot was thinking of revenge.

He was undoubtedly brooding over it, and trying to cudgel his poor wits until they told him what to do, and how best to enjoy the vengeance for which he panted.

An ill-conditioned, ill-regulated, diseased mind is sure to dwell upon vengeance whenever its owner has been, in the slightest degree, slighted or irritated.

There is no thing large or generous in such a mind

It does not know how to forgive.

It cannot stoop to be merciful and generous.

All it can mumble is, "An eye for an eye, and a tooth for tooth!" which is cruel and savage.

Rather should it be intent upon returning good for evil, for then it might hope for forgiveness on that dread day of final reckoning.

"Do you know the lake shore?" asked Hunston of the idiot.

"I know all the country round."

"Then go the most direct road to South-beach."

"That'll be through the Devil's Gap."

"Very well."

As he pronounced the name his eyes flashed, and he seemed at length to have grasped an idea which was flitting about his mind like a little bird around a corn-rick.

He put himself by the head of the donkey, while Hunston walked behind, and the cavalcade set off at a slow space.

Hunston endeavoured to persuade the donkey to move a little quicker by belabouring it with a thick ash plant, but the creature's hide seemed to be impervious to blows, and it merely whisked its tail, as if a troublesome gad-fly was paying unpleasant attention to it.

Hunston was profoundly ignorant of the nature of the country through which he was passing.

So elated was he at this prospect that he trod upon air.

He neither looked to the right nor to the left of him.

He carried his head high in the air as if he was already the monarch of all he surveyed, dwelt in marble halls, and had vassals and serfs by his side.

Slinking Sammy watched Hunston carefully, and did not fail to notice how unusually preoccupied he was.

Ever and anon his vigilant eye— usually so dozy, so lustreless, and so expressionless, now flashing unwonted fire and eloquence of anger—allowed its gaze to fall upon Hunston.

Then it wandered back again, and marked out the way.

It was a singular fact that the idiot was going in the direction of the Devil's Gap—an eccentric freak of nature, a dangerous gully, an unfathomable gulf.

He neared it gradually, and when he got within a few yards of it he drew a ragged handkerchief from his pocket and fastened it over the donkey's eyes.

Hunston was so absorbed in his own thoughts that all this was totally lost to him.

He thought that the journey to the South-beach, where Fannie was waiting for him, could not be accomplished under a certain time, and that the idiot would not dare to mislead him, after the jacketing he had given him in the morning.

So he gave himself up to meditation, and felt supremely happy in making plans for the future.

Slinking Sammy caused the donkey to go straight toward the Devil's Gap.

The animal, unsuspicious of danger, stepped boldly out.

The idiot fell behind a few paces.

Then there was a crash, a cry, and donkey, barrow, and gold, were precipitated into the abyss.

The idiot took to his heels, and ran with in-

The tracks of bears, however, were distinctly visible.

He dropped down about two feet and a half, and peered under a huge rock.

Two fierce black eyes met his, and they glared upon him like live coals.

Instantly he levelled his rifle, which he carried in the hollow of his arm ready for use.

There was a report.

Then a blinding smoke arose, and the next thing he knew was that a heavy body precipitated itself upon him, and he was borne to the earth. With a quickness born of despair he drew his knife and plunged it into the mass which had attacked him.

Sharp, acute pain ran through his shoulders, and he felt that something was encircling him with the deathly grasp of an anaconda.

That he was in the grasp of a grizzly bear he couldn't doubt.

As soon as the bear relaxed its grasp of Jack, a feeling as if hot water was running over him gave way to the horrible sense of suffocation from which he had been suffering.

The grip relaxed.

He could breathe again.

Making a gigantic effort he threw off the incumbent weight and rose to his feet.

Dashing the snow and blood from his eyes, he saw that he was in front of a cavern.

It was not of wide dimensions, but formed a snug retreat for any wild animal.

Before him were two cubs, standing uneasily at the mouth of the cave and making strange noises.

At his feet was a huge bear.

His bullet had struck it, but not in a vital part, and it would have gone hard with him if he had not used his knife to good advantage.

The bear was stabbed to the heart, and appeared to be quite dead. As for himself, Jack had escaped with a few scratches, which, though smarting and painful, were not serious.

"Helloa! down thar!" exclaimed Hank.

"All right above?" asked Jack.

"Ye-a."

"Same here. I've killed a bear, and if I'm not mistaken it is a prime one."

Mr. Mole peeped over the edge of the pit.

"Yes, indeed!" he exclaimed. "It is a very fine specimen of the *genus*; let us call him *Ursa Major*. Well done, Jack! Now we shall have bear meat."

"See any cubs inside, cap?" asked Hank.

"Two," replied Jack.

"Wal, let 'em stay till to-morrow. The old father's away for food, and he'll mind them. We'll skin and cut up this one, and have time enough to attend to the rest of the family after a while."

Jack drew his knife across the bear's throat to make sure that the formidable beast was dead, and Hank jumped down to join him.

"Air yer hurt, kernel?" he inquired.

"Just a little. Not much. Nothing of any account," replied Jack.

"I only asked because I see you was bleeding. I tell you it was a big thing to tackle that b'ar the way you did. B'ars is mighty ugly varmints when they've got young, and, it's no use a-talkin, you're gritty, or you would not have done it and come out so well."

Hank took the measure of the bear.

"As fine a grizzly as ever I see," he continued; "and you struck him jest in the right place. See here. Touched the heart, sure."

"It was more by accident than anything else," replied Jack, modestly, though he was pleased with the old man's praise.

"No, no. You knew where to strike him, but, like all the real good ones, you don't talk much. Trumpeters aren't much account. The man as does great things never blows his own trumpet, and you know it."

"I believe you're right there, Hank," said Jack. "Though, on this occasion, I was perhaps more lucky than I deserved to be, for you must admit I did a foolhardy thing in jumping down into the bear's cave."

"Yer did that."

"Sort of thing you would not have done yourself—eh?"

"No," said Hank. "You couldn't have hired me to do it, though I'm no coward. No, kernel, I'd hev routed the b'ar rather than hev called at his house and left my card on him, as you did. Civility of that kind is thrown away upon b'ars, and they don't appreciate our high-toned civilisation."

Jack smiled.

"Now, cl'ar out of here!" said Hank, drawing his knife, "and give a fellow elbow-room to swing a cat. I'm going to cut up that b'ar right away, and we'll take home all the meat we can carry, and hide the rest till next day, when we'll slaughter the cubs, too."

"Good enough, Hank. I've done my share, though I'll lend you a hand in cutting up the meat, if you like."

"You will—not," said Hank. "It's my trade, and I don't want no apprentices to-day."

In obedience to this request, which was given in a tone of command peculiar to the hunter when there was any business which he deemed of importance to be transacted, Jack climbed up the sides of the gully, and rejoined his companions.

"Golly! Marse Jack!" cried Monday. "We thought you was gone, sure, when um bear got out at you. We all going to shoot, but couldn't get a chance, and we might as well have killed you as the bear. Um both roll over and over, till we couldn't tell which was Marse Jack and which was the bear."

"Thank you, Monday," replied Jack; "I'm not hurt."

"Bleedin', though."

"It's more the bear's blood than mine, though I expect I present rather a formidable appearance, torn and blood-stained as I am."

"We've been through worse than that, Marse Jack, and we come out all right, eh?"

"Yes, we've been tolerably lucky," answered Jack.

"I don't see," remarked Mr. Mole, "that there is anything very wonderful in killing a poor bear. The animal is unarmed, and the hunter attacks him with rifle and knife. What chance has the unhappy beast? It is ten to one on the man."

Jack had his back turned to the Professor.

He was looking over the wide expanse of frozen snow.

Suddenly something arrested his attention.

It was coming along at a shambling gait, but moving rapidly, nevertheless.

His practised eye—for Jack had now a pretty good experience on the plains—told him that it was a bear.

Probably the he-bear coming home to his she and cubs with some food that he had been out foraging for.

Turning round, he exclaimed—

"You may despise the bear, and bet on the man, sir, but here is a chance of proving your argument. See what is coming!"

Mr. Mole put his glass in his eye.

"No," he answered. "I frankly admit that I do not."

"Can you see nothing?"

"A black speck on the snow."

"That is a bear."

"Really?"

"Yes. And I bet you a hundred pounds to your old boots that he is the master of the cave. You have now a good opportunity of showing us how easily the man can kill the bear."

"I?"

"You are armed, rifle and knife, and I observe a tomahawk at your belt."

"Ye-es," replied Mole; "a rather a fancy sort of article, which I could not depend upon much."

"But your rifle is loaded?"

"Oh, yes."

"And you can shoot with it?"

"You know I can," said Mole, indignantly.

"Very well. Sail in on that coming bear and show us what the man can do against the beast."

The Professor looked very uncomfortable, but he raised his rifle and sighted for a long shot.

"Lie on your back and cock up one knee," said Harvey.

"Oh, let um alone," said Monday. "Mr. Mole know how to do dis ting."

The Professor fired, the bullet going fifty yards wide of the mark.

On came the bear.

"Couldn't hit a haystack at point-blank distance," said Harvey.

Mr. Mole threw his rifle down in disgust.

"If I am to be chaffed at by a parcel of hobble-de-hoys, who are neither boys nor men," he said, "it is time for me to let them show what they can do"

"Don't get nasty, sir," said Harvey.

"But I am nasty. You made me so. Shoot bears yourself. The best shot may miss sometimes. I will go and leave you and your bear. Perhaps you won't do anything better than I did."

He walked away in a high state of bad temper, and hid himself behind one of the rocks.

"Scared out of his life," said Harvey.

"You may bet on that," said Jack.

"Shall I have a go at the bear?" continued Harvey. "You killed one. Let me have this."

"Why certainly. I'll back you up in case your shot misses. Go for the heart. A bear is as difficult to kill as a cat or a rabbit. Bears carry the lead a long way."

"See me drop him in his tracks," answered Harvey.

He took a careful aim and fired.

The bear was within a hundred and fifty yards of him and apparently savagely running to drive the intruders out of the bit of ground he had selected for his winter home.

The shot struck him, and made him stagger for a moment.

But he did not appear to be seriously injured.

"Fire, fire, Jack!" cried Harvey, "while I slip in another cartridge."

Jack, however, did not follow his advice.

He waited for the bear to come nearer, his rifle in rest, and his quick, bright eye watching every movement of the advancing animal.

At length he deemed the distance short enough to enable him to put a bullet in the brain, and he fired.

But just as he did so, the bear, which had been injured by Harvey's shot, stumbled, causing the bullet to fly wide of its mark.

On came the bear.

"Look out!" cried Jack. "Get behind the rock and give him the contents of your pistol, Dick."

Both young men fired their revolvers, but the bullets seemed to have no effect on the bear.

Jack wished he had some explosive bullets, which are more destructive than the ordinary leaden ones.

He ran in one direction, and Harvey in the other, but they met under the rock which had given shelter to Mr. Mole.

The Professor at first could not account for their presence.

"What is the matter?" he asked.

"Missed the bear, that's all," answered Jack, "and we had to take shelter while we loaded again"

"Ha! ha! It is my turn to laugh now," replied Mr. Mole. "You fellows were bragging about what you could do, and yet the pair of you — bark me, the pair of you—could not kill one paltry bear."

"If you think you can, there is a chance for you, sir," replied Harvey. "He's around the premises somewhere."

"No, thank you," answered Mole, "not now. I never like interfering in a bungled and botched affair. If I'd started on it at first, I'd have carried it through. By-the-way, did you warn Hank of the danger?"

"By Jove!" said Harvey, "I forgot that."

"So did I," remarked Jack.

"How silly!" continued the Professor. "Of course the he-bear will make for the cave where he left his she with the young ones, and I expect he will not be in the best of humours after the imbecile way in which you have been tickling him with pistol-balls."

"Are you loaded up?" asked Harvey of Jack.

"Yes," was the reply.

They looked at one another and dashed out over the snow to see what they could do for Hank, blaming themselves for not having warned him, and hoping that he had not been taken unawares.

Monday was nowhere to be seen, and there was just the chance that he might have joined Hank to assist in cutting up the bear.

As they approached the cave, the sounds of men engaged in a fierce struggle were heard.

It was evident that a terrible conflict was going on.

Jack peered over the side of the pit, and beheld a black heap on the ensanguined snow.

Sometimes it was half man, then half bear, then two-thirds man and one-third bear.

Blood flowed like water, and fearful oaths were mingled with savage grunts.

Without a moment's hesitation Jack jumped into the pit.

He felt for the bear's ear, and putting his revolver in it, fired off five chambers in quick succession.

The bear began to stiffen out and gave convulsive kicks.

Harvey now joined Jack, and between them they pulled the bear, which was dead enough, on one side.

It was the largest they had ever seen.

But the bear did not interest them so much as did the sight they saw beneath it.

Hank Smith and Monday were lying one on his back, the other face downward, and the snow about them was literally honeycombed by the rush of hot blood from bear and man, which still smoked and seamed like the gutter of a slaughterhouse.

"Are you hurt, Hank?" asked Jack, raising him up.

"I'm rather frightened, kernel, if I ain't chawed up," answered Hank; "though, to be truthful, I can't tell yet how much I'm hurt, and I'd like to get up and see if there's any bones broken."

Jack assisted him to rise.

"I'm scratched and bit," continued Hank, "but don't feel much damage done, though there's no saying what might hev happened if you hadn't come up as yer did. How was it that the b'ar passed you without yer seeing of it and giving the alarm? You might hev knowed it would dash straight's a bee-line for its home."

"We fired at it and retreated to load, quite forgetting you."

"It ain't good to forget these things, boyee, and many a man's left his bones out here through he or his friends not keeping their heads on a level. When that b'ar came down on me I thought I was a goner. He seemed to kinder hev a knowledge that I was carving his wife. Never expected nothin' of the sort. The coon had jes jined me —Thunderation! I'd omitted to think of him. Why, he is lying on his face. Send he aren't dead."

This exclamation, which the garrulous hunter uttered in the midst of his speech, turned general attention to Monday.

He appeared to be insensible.

Jack turned him over, and though he breathed it was with difficulty.

"The coon's got it bad," exclaimed Hank. "Let's hev a feel of him all over, and see where he is hurted."

They all three examined the Malay's body, but could find no bites and no scratches.

"That's odd," said Jack.

"Very strange, indeed," said Harvey.

"I know how 'tis, fellows," exclaimed Hank, as he bared his arm and showed a place above the elbow where the flesh had been chewed and scratched till it resembled raw meat torn about by a cat.

"Oh!" said Jack, "that's a bad place."

"I'll bet you it is; but you wait till I put a snow bandage on it. That will ease the smartin' and keep down the inflammation, though I'll hev to wear this arm in a sling for a month, and won't get much sleep for the present. A chawed arm is worse than a six-week's-old baby of extra double squalling power."

"But about Monday!" exclaimed Jack. "Is he dead?"

"Not he. Tell yer how it was, kernel. When the bear lighted on us, he gave Monday the first hug and then began to chaw me. The coon got the best of that deal. He's lost considerable wind, but soon's he comes to he'll be all right."

"That hug is a dangerous thing," said Jack, shaking his head.

He looked at Monday with apprehension, but to his delight, the black opened his eyes and cast a glance around him.

"Who's that take the liberty of hugging me?" he asked. "Um never feel such a thing before. Thought my head was going into um stomach, and um stomach into um boots. Oh, golly, Marse Jack, don't bring me out to kill no more bears!"

"We can afford to laugh now it is all over," said Jack. "But we have all had narrow escapes, and I am sorry to say that Hank has suffered more severely than any of us."

"It's all in the day's work, cap," replied Hank.

"You must excuse me from active duty, that's all!"

"Certainly. Tell us what meat to carry home, and we'll shoulder it. Can you handle your gun?"

"Yes. One hand will do for that"

In a short time the meat was packed, and a certain weight apportioned to each.

The remainder of the she-bear and the whole carcase of the other was put in the cave with the cubs, and secured from intruders by two heavy stones which were rolled up against the entrance, effectually concealing it.

Hank was regarding his knife somewhat angrily.

"I've lost confidence in this knife," he remarked. "It didn't stick that b'ar a bit. I jabbed at him more'n ha'f a dozen times and couldn't make him feel. Now, it don't pay to keep a dog and bark yourself, so I'll change knives with eer a one of you boys."

"Perhaps you didn't get a chance to stick him in a vital part," said Jack.

"My hand war kinder cramped, that's true, and b'ars is awful hard to kill. Well, I guess I won't change this knife. It's done good work for me, and stripped off a pile of skins when I've started on the plains."

When all was in readiness, and even the Professor was burdened with his share of the fresh meat, the party started for home.

It was clear and frosty.

They had no difficulty in retracing their steps, as the tracks they had made in coming were still plainly visible in the snow.

"We've had quite a big hunt," said Harvey.

"Yes, indeed," replied Jack, "and I have quite a big appetite."

"I hope Hilda will have kept in a good fire."

"So do I"

"She and Monday will do the cooking, while you and I attend to poor old Hank's arm. Eh?"

"Yes, it must be doctored. It's very bad, and I'll bet very painful, but the old man has so much true grit in him that he wouldn't squeal if his flesh was taken off his bones bit by bit," said Jack.

"That' so. I never saw a man bear pain better," replied Harvey.

The sun had set when they came once more under the shadow of the Black Hills, whose pine-covered sides were on this occasion whitened with the snow, but the wind had shaken the bleached mantle off the boughs and trunks of the dark trees, whose sombre foliage imparted a funereal aspect to the scene.

To the surprise of the hunters, no cheering fire was blazing.

Only some smouldering embers remained to show where the fire had been.

"Why, how's this?" exclaimed Harvey. "Hilda's let the fire out."

This was no joke for hungry men coming home with fresh meat.

"Perhaps she felt sick, and has gone to sleep," suggested Jack.

Harvey ran on ahead, and cried "Hilda! Hilda! Where are you?"

A dull, cavernous echo sent back the words.

This was the only response.

Again and again Harvey called his wife without any further result.

His face paled.

He trembled in every limb as he advanced to search the tents.

His heart misgave him.

muttering as he went—

"If Sammy is not to have the gold, *he shan't* have it! No one beats Sammy for nothing. He will have his revenge—oh, yes! Revenge is better than gold. It is sweeter than gold, and Sammy likes it best."

When the state of the case revealed itself to Hunston, he uttered a terrible outcry.

The blood rushed to his head, and he was as one stunned.

The suddenness of the great calamity which had befallen him nearly deprived him of his senses.

He cursed, and swore, and raved like a madman, and crawled to the edge of the chasm, thinking that he might discover his bags of gold at the bottom, but all was black as night, and he rose up blaspheming and cursing the hour in which he was born.

All his dreams had been dashed to atoms like so much fragile and brittle glass.

All his visions had vanished.

He was utterly bankrupt!

And by whom had his complete bankruptcy been caused.

By whom had he been so completely prostrated and cast down?

By an idiot, a rascally, half-witted fellow, whose neck he regretted not having broken.

He bitterly lamented his leniency.

He had shed blood before, and he was only sorry to think that he had refrained from doing so now.

Regrets, however, were useless.

The money was gone.

He threw himself on the grass, and bit the herbage with his teeth, tearing his hair, meanwhile, in his frantic rage.

Had Slinking Sammy fallen into Hunston's power at that moment, he would most assuredly have followed the gold down the Devil's Gap.

At length Hunston roused himself to a sense of the situation.

Getting up, he peered over the jagged and precipitous sides of the Devil's Gap.

It had been aptly named by the miners.

Its black, cavernous recesses, down which the rippling water passed, seemed, indeed, to have been the work of the Evil One.

"No use in trying to get back that gold," he exclaimed, with a shake of the head. "That is gone, past redemption—worse luck! Well, there is plenty more in the earth, and I dare say I can get on without it."

In this philosophical state of mind he hastily traversed the short distance which remained between him and the beach.

It was not yet dark.

The boat was lying high and dry upon the sand, and Fannie was pacing up and down, as if impatient at being kept waiting so long.

Whether this was so or not, she did not evince any signs of ill-temper, for she ran forward to Hunston, and, throwing herself into his arms, pressed her lips to his, murmuring—

"My dear, dear husband!"

"My darling!" exclaimed Hunston, returning her caress, and disengaging himself from her embrace.

"Where's the gold?" she asked.

"Gone!"

"Where?"

"Down the Devil's Gap—an infernal gully about two miles from here. I found the bags safe but there's many a slip 'twixt the cup and the lip, and you'll have to do without the fortune I promised you on your wedding-day, Fannie."

She smiled.

"You are all the fortune I want, dear," she said; "but tell me all about it."

He related all that had occurred, and dwelt particularly upon the skilfully planned villainy of Slinking Sammy.

"The half-witted," said Fannie, "are usually treacherous, because their minds are not equally balanced. He wants ballast, poor fellow."

"I'll ballast him with an ounce of lead if ever we meet again."

"Of course you are annoyed, and I don't wonder at it. But I'd think of something else. Shall we make a start, dear?"

"I am willing," said Hunston. "Get aboard."

Fannie entered the boat, and Hunston, shoving her off, followed, pleased to think that Fannie bore her disappointment much better than he had expected she would.

CHAPTER XIII.

A MADDENING MYSTERY.

THE spot which Harkaway had selected for his camp is easily described.

It was situated in the heart of the island in the lake.

On the eastern side was a long range of hills, which almost deserved the name of mountains.

He had chosen high ground.

Close to where he had pitched his tent was a running stream, which descended from the hills and ran with such velocity that, even when it froze hard, the water did not congeal, though lumps of ice came down with the current.

In the immediate vicinity was a cavernous fissure in the earth, about twenty-five by fifteen feet in size.

The edges were rough and jagged.

Its depth was a matter of conjecture, but Professor Mole, who had recovered from his illness, undertook to explore it, and dropping stones down, could hear no sound, and so he judged it to be unfathomable.

He spent two whole days examining the crevice.

At length he gave his opinion.

"The island, Harkaway," he said, "is evidently of volcanic origin. I find traces in every direction to support this view."

"Well, sir," replied Jack, "what do you think of the ash-pit?"

He had christened the deep hole close by them the ash-pit, because they had been in the habit, during their brief stay there, of throwing all their refuse down the chasm.

"That is one of the numerous mouths of an extinct volcano."

"A crater?"

"Precisely. Not the grand one, but an outlet formed during some magnificent eruption."

"Of late years?"

"No, sir," said Mr. Mole. "I should imagine that when these mountains were in active eruption, it was in the age of prehistoric man."

"Let's take a look at it," said Jack.

They had not far to go.

The huge pit was yawning, black and dismal, within a dozen paces of the white, gleaming tents which constituted the camp.

He had a foreboding of coming trouble.

The tents were empty.

No trace of Hilda was to be discovered.

He rejoined the party, and exclaimed "My wife is not here!"

Hank looked carefully round.

"That's tarnation strange," he said. "I can't see any tracks of Injuns round about: there's only our own footmarks."

"Couldn't they cover up their trail?" asked Jack.

"Not well enough to deceive me, guv'nor."

"It's your opinion that no one has visited the ranche during our absence?"

"Don't see no signs of it."

"Where can she have gone?"

"That's the mystery."

Harvey sat down, completely stupefied.

What could have become of Hilda?

That was the maddening mystery which perplexed the minds of all of them.

CHAPTER XIV.

MORE VICTIMS OF THE UNKNOWN.

ANOTHER and still more minute and diligent search for Hilda was started within the precincts of the camp.

But without success.

The snow without lay untrodden, as we have said, save where the hunting-party had quitted it in the morning and re-entered it in the evening.

No trace of the missing woman could be discovered.

In no direction were there any signs of Indians or others.

If Hilda had been forcibly carried off, the surrounding snow would have told a tale, for it would have been impossible for any body of men, or any single man, even, to have removed her without leaving some indication of violence behind him or them.

Harvey was nearly distracted.

He could now tell what Harkaway had suffered in being deprived of the society of his dearly loved companion.

But he bore his trouble bravely, and beyond a careworn and haggard expression, and a preoccupied and nervous manner, did not betray the emotion which he really felt.

The others sat down to supper, though their efforts to induce him to touch anything were fruitless.

He could not eat a morsel of food.

There are times of mental excitement when the body lives on itself, as it were, and disdains nourishment of any kind.

Hank, however, made a prodigious meal, devouring at least four pounds of the bear.

"How much longer are you going on, Hank?" inquired Jack. "There must be a limit to your capacity."

"I'm done, kernel," replied Hank, "and I'll admit that I've made a hog of myself, which is a thing I don't often do."

"I am glad," said Mr. Mole, "that you have the decency to admit it, for anything more disgusting than the way in which you have gorged yourself I never saw."

"Hold on now, Pro-fessor," cried Hank. "Let me have my say. I've worked hard to-day; considerable harder 'n you, and I've lost blood; the system has to be kep' up."

"So has Harkaway been wounded, so has Monday, and they did not make such a revolting exhibition of themselves."

"What's that?"

"You're a beast," said Mr. Mole.

"That's calling names, but when I look at the source it comes from, it's like water fallin' off a duck's back. Go ahead, Pro-fessor; favour us with a little more."

"You should put a curb on your appetite."

"And you should put a bridle on your tongue. I could lick you easy if I had a mind to."

"That's the resort of the brutal and uneducated. Just what I expected; when a man finds himself beaten in argument he has recourse to his fists."

"Hush up, sir," cried Jack. "We don't want to wrangle when we ought to be sympathizing with Harvey, and trying to unravel this maddening mystery."

"I am silent, Jack," replied Mr Mole, "only this man attacked me first, with his usual volubility of tongue and indecent haste."

"Wall, I never did," said Hank.

"Never did what?" said Mr. Mole.

"Never see the like of you. I can't go in for fine talk and big words like you, but to say that I had the vollem—vollem—what was it?—to go for you first, and——"

"Hank, will you be quiet?" said Jack, interrupting him.

"It's hard, kernel."

"To oblige me."

"I'd do most anything to oblige you, but it's rough to be called names by the Professor, and to be backbitten, too. I wouldn't like to say he's a liar, but I think so."

"That will do."

"I laugh at him," said Mr. Mole.

"And I la'f at you. I have to la'f," replied Hank. "I'd like to skin you, same as I did the b'ar, and send your hide to the museum, where they show the hyenas, and the gorillas, and such like."

"When I appear in such a place, you'll be there, my friend."

"They'll give you a glass case all to yourself, and label you the champion fraud," replied Hank.

"And you will be the unique specimen of the frontier nonsuch."

"Is it worthy of you, sir," said Jack, "to keep up this chaff?"

"I have had to chaff bargemen in my time, Jack, and why not backwoodsmen?"

"But——"

"Ask him to leave off. He shan't have the last word."

"You're worse than an old woman, sir, after her tenth cup of tea."

"He licks all creation," said Hank; "and if I were you, kernel, I'd bounce him down what he calls the crater."

"Ha!" suddenly ejaculated Harvey.

"What's the matter?" inquired Jack.

"That remark of Hank's has given me an idea," replied Harvey.

"How?"

"Could Hilda have fallen down that big hole? You know how tidy she was, never liking to see anything lying about, and she might have, putting things straight, swept up a little straw, and gone to the crater, the side might have given way, and—you catch the idea?"

"Perfectly."

"I wish it was daylight; we'd explore."

"Even then, you would see nothing," said Jack. "I don't suppose for a moment she has fallen down, though if she had, there would be no sign of it."

follow. Be careful, all of you. Can't afford to have this day marred by any accident."

"Not much, governor," said Young Jack.

With great care, Hilda and Viola were raised to the surface.

Soon all the members of the party were on the surface ground.

Then there was such running about, laughing, hand-shaking, mutual congratulation, eating and drinking, as had never been seen in those regions before.

Jack's delight at recovering his wife and child was unbounded.

He was once more surrounded by his friends, and his enemy, Hunston, was a wounded captive in his hands.

But he did not forget the mission which had brought him into the heart of the Black Hills.

He was in search of the Mountain of Gold and the Secret of Wealth.

No alchemist of the Middle Ages trying to transmute base metals into gold, or endeavouring to discover the elixir of life, was more anxious than he to bring his efforts to a successful issue.

The prophecy of Mir-a-ma, and the mysterious words of the ill-fated Pe-bo-a, all led him to believe that he was on the verge of a startling event.

As soon as the excitement consequent on the reunion of the party had passed away, he took Dick Harvey on one side.

"Will you go down into the Kehamas with me?" he asked.

"Why, certainly I will," said Harvey.

"I am firmly of opinion that in the bosom of these hills will be found the Secret of Wealth."

"Gold, you mean?"

"Mountains of it," replied Jack.

"I don't know about that," said Harvey, shaking his head. "We may find mountains of auriferous quartz, but hills of pure virgin gold are too much to expect."

"Let us go and see. Call Monday."

Monday was soon in attendance.

"Whatium want, sah?" he asked.

"Go and cut some pine-knots - as many as you can carry," replied Jack.

"All right, sah. See um heap there. Hank cut them. Couldn't be served quicker in a barber-shop on Sunday morning, when you're number seventy-nine, and seventy-eight in the chair."

Monday made up a bundle of pine-knots, and the trio descended into the Kehamas, which had until so recently been the abode of Pe-bo-a.

A melancholy silence reigned throughout.

The darkness of the grave prevailed.

With lighted torches they wandered from chamber to chamber, their wonder and admiration increasing at every step they took.

Never had they heard of hills being so honeycombed as were these.

In order to secure their retreat, and prevent the chance of being lost in the vast maze, they cut notches in the walls, at intervals, with a tomahawk.

At each turning they made a cross.

All at once they entered the largest cavern they had yet visited.

The whole of one side was filled with rudely-cut stone coffins.

"I'll tell you," replied Jack. "The Indians who formerly roamed over these hills knew all about the Secret of Wealth, but they would never reveal it to the outside world, for fear the white men should come and drive them away."

"Well?"

"So they left some records or instructions respecting it in this place."

"All right," said Harvey, with a smile. "You are welcome to your opinion."

"I know it is so."

"You are crazy on this point," continued Harvey.

"Dick," said Jack, almost angry, "I am sorry I brought you here."

"Kick me out, then."

"I've a good mind to."

Jack playfully gave him a push.

He stumbled up against Monday and sent him rolling against a pile of coffins.

The shock caused the top one to fall with a crash, and the lid came off.

A cloud of dust arose.

Jack held his torch aloft and looked on curiously.

"That stone harder than um head," said Monday.

"What's that thing?" said Harvey.

He pointed to a parchment scroll which was visible as the dust began to settle.

Jack ran forward and grasped it eagerly.

He held it up.

It was covered with writing.

"Hold a light, Dick!" he exclaimed. "Here, Monday, come on the other side. Hurry."

They stood one on each side of him.

He unrolled the scroll.

The writing was in English, and inscribed in a round, plain, monastic hand.

It ran as follows—

"This is the burying-place of the King of the Tribes. I, Manuel Quesada, a Jesuit priest and Catholic missionary, born in Spain, but having become the companion of King Philip in his wanderings, do take down his last words for the benefit of posterity, if in time to come this scroll shall be brought to light:

"Metamora,

"(called King Philip by the settlers),

"Chief of the Wampanoags,

"says as follows to his people:

"Ye who would learn the Secret of Wealth, attend to these words:

"1. Seek not after vain, worldly pleasures, and gold and silver, which are as dross.

"2. Love the Great Spirit and obey His laws.

"3. Honour thy father and thy mother, for they cared for thee when thou couldst not help thyself.

"4. Do unto all others as you would be done unto.

"5. Love thy neighbour as thyself.

"6. Owe no man anything.

"7. Be kind, obliging, temperate in all things, rising and retiring early, shun evil companions, respect those around you who deserve respect, be not led away by foolish thoughts. Think more of home than outdoor life, and live always in such a manner that when your end comes—as come it must—you may exclaim:

"'O, Great Spirit!

"'I go to the mansion of the blest!'

with a violence that jarred up both his arms.

Taking the spade, he cleared the earth away, and came to a slab of roughly-hewn sandstone.

That this was the slab mentioned in the manuscript he had little doubt, and he laboured with redoubled ardour.

He at length succeeded in forcing it from its resting-place, and with a Herculean effort threw it upon the bank of the pit he had been digging.

Then came the investigation.

He lighted a lantern he had brought with him, and saw, by its aid, that he had opened a small hole, in which several canvas bags were lying, one on top of the other.

For a moment he stood mute with rapture and ecstasy.

He had found the treasure.

When the first feeling of joy wore off, he stooped down and grasped one of the bags, intending to throw it on the ground and examine it.

As he touched the covering, it broke.

The canvas had worn out, and was as rotten as so much tissue-paper.

The gold poured out in a stream, and fell, with a ringing sound, upon the ground.

He took some of the nuggets in his hand and felt them, bit them, and otherwise tested them.

They were gold—good, solid gold.

The manuscript did not lie, for he had found a veritable treasure.

Having learnt caution and prudence by the rupture of the bag, he took hold of the others carefully, with both hands, supporting the weight on his palms, and deposited them, one after the other, on the floor of the old hut.

Hunston's delight was intense.

During the whole of his existence, he had never experienced such delight.

To find a treasure, as he had done, was to realise the dream of his youth.

It was to substantiate the visions of his boyhood, which he had all along considered to be too brightened and too brilliant for credence.

As he placed bag after bag, heavy and loaded with gold, upon the brink of the chasm, he smiled with a grand joy, for he felt that he was making his fortune in a wonderful manner.

The bags of gold were forty-two in number.

He stood over them and counted them; and as he counted them, he held his spade upraised, so as to brain anyone who interrupted his agreeable and congenial occupation.

Having satisfied himself that his enumeration was correct, he jumped lightly into the grave, and proceeded to pick up some lumps which had fallen out of the first bag, which he had the misfortune to break.

He threw them on the bank in a heap.

The task occupied some time.

All this, if he could only convey it away secretly, was his own

He fell back against the freshly-disturbed earth, overcome by the violence of his emotions, and reflected on the singularity of his destiny, which raised him in one day from a subordinate position to one of prosperity and independence.

This was the dead miner's hoard, and well worth finding it proved.

Hunston drew a handkerchief from his pocket, and wiped the perspiration from his forehead.

Suddenly a weird laugh aroused his attention.

He looked up and saw a little stumpy, half-grown fellow sitting on his bags of gold.

"Ha, ha! hey, hey! ho, ho!" laughed the

covery which it had been his good fortune to make.

He was a singular creature, well known at the Gap.

He was ill-shapen, but his senses were acute enough, and Hunston had feared him when he first spoke to him that morning.

His name was Sammy, and he had acquired the prefix of "Slinking," as we have already said, owing to a habit he had of slinking about and prying into other people's affairs.

No one ever heard him approach them.

His motions were noiseless, and those upon whom he obtruded himself were only aware of his presence when the fellow was upon them.

"Ho, ho! Mr. Hunston I heard your name from Tom Wanzer, and I've followed you," exclaimed Slinking Sammy. "What are you going to do with all tha goold?"

Hunston glared at him without making any reply, but the restless way in which he moved his hands showed that he was fully prepared to protect his property, newly acquired though it was, even if Slinking Sammy's life had to be sacrificed in the endeavour.

At first Hunston felt very considerably annoyed at the intrusion of the idiot upon what he considered his privacy.

He could see that though the poor fellow's mind was diseased, it was not utterly gone.

Some sense remained.

Had it not been so, he would not have made the remark that he did about the gold

He did not know what to do with him

To knock him on the head with a shovel, and place him in the hole afterwards, shovelling the earth over his miserable carcase, would be easy enough.

But the emergency was scarcely sufficiently pressing for the adoption of so violent a method of getting rid of a troublesome companion.

Hunston leant on his spade and mused.

Slinking Sammy's eyes were riveted on the gold in a fascinated manner.

The glittering lumps seemed to have the utmost attraction for him.

He ran his hand through the heap which Hunston had accumulated on the ground, and listened rapturously to the noise they made in falling upon one another.

Then he scooped up a handful, and raising them, allowed them to fall on his head, neck, and shoulders

Occasionally, when he thought Hunston was not looking, he would, with a sly, cunning smile, slip a few pieces into his pockets and up his sleeves, his eyes twinkling the while, as if he were intensely excited in a most pleasurable manner.

At length Hunston looked up.

He had resolved to use no violence towards the idiot.

He considered that his best policy was one of conciliation.

Slinking Sammy was a strong, powerful fellow, stoutly knit and well put together. Why not make use of him?

For many reasons, Hunston did not wish to go back to Flyaway Gap with his treasure.

It was his desire to pack up the gold and convey it to the boat without a soul being aware of his sudden acquisition of wealth.

When Thomas Wanzer accosted him, as he would, if they should meet again, and asked him what luck he had met with, he intended to reply in a desponding tone, and declare that he had had his labour for nothing.

" You shall stop at home to-morrow when we go out after more bear-meat."

" That will suit my complaint exactly. You'll find me here."

" It's all very well to be brave and laugh at these mysterious disappearances, but what is your theory ?"

" My theory ?"

" Yes."

" I have formed one, and I'll give it you," answered the Professor. " Give it you cheerfully, but I do not expect you to believe me, though you must admit it is plausible."

" Let's hear it."

Everyone looked inquiringly at Mr. Mole.

" It's my idea," he said, " that Hilda fell down the crater accidentally, and that Harvey, all alone by himself, cold and miserable, loving his wife as we know he did, lost all command over himself, and committed suicide by throwing himself after her."

" Dick wouldn't do it," said Jack.

" How do you know ?" replied Mr. Mole. " Because you have a hard head and very little feeling. Why judge everybody else by your standard ?"

" I've more feeling in my little finger than you have in your whole body, you old fossil," answered Jack.

" That's right ; abuse me. It's the fashion in this camp to abuse me. To the deuce with Western life, say I if this is to be the style day after day. Call me more names. Revile me some more, wont you ?"

" Oh ! I don't want to have any fuss with you."

" You can't, if you try. I am too even-tempered a man for that, and can always make allowances for the champagney effervescence,' of youth."

Hank looked at Jack.

" If he called me a ' champagney effervescence,' I'd have come for him," he remarked.

" Oh ! let him go on," replied Jack. " We shan't see him after to-morrow."

" Won't you ! That's all you know. I sleep with one eye open. You don't catch this weasel asleep. No, sir," answered Mr. Mole.

Jack walked up and down impatiently, while Hank and Monday, as usual, set about preparing the supper.

The aspect affairs were assuming was a serious one.

He did not like it at all.

If he had an open, palpable enemy to fight, it would make all the difference in the world.

But he was fighting in the dark.

Could these strange vanishings be the work of Hunston ?

It was possible, and yet he could not see how the work could be carried out with no trace of the workmen being left behind.

The more he thought, the more perplexed he grew.

That night passed as the one before had done Hank and Monday divided the watches between them.

But nothing occurred to disturb them.

In the morning, Mr. Mole was resolute in his resolve to stay alone.

" Don't weaken any, professor ?" said Hank.

" Not a little bit," replied Mr. Mole.

" Wal, I'll take a tearful adoo of yer, never expecting to see yer agin. Good-by, Pro-fessor. I hope they won't make it red-hot whar you going to !"

" Anyhow" answered Mr. Mole, " I shall have

the consolation of knowing that you will join me some day."

" Don't yer bet on it," said Hank.

They gave him a supply of whisky, and saw that his rifle and pistols were in good order.

Then they started once more for the bear's cave.

Only three of them, now.

Hank, Jack, and Monday.

" This reminds me of the old German story of the iron room," said Jack, as they walked along.

" What was that, kernel ?" said Hank. " I never hear tell of it."

" A man was imprisoned in a mechanically contrived room, which had seven windows. He went to sleep, and when he woke up in the morning and looked round, he found there were only six."

" Only six ?" repeated Hank.

" That was all."

" I want to know."

" You see, the machinery was put in motion while the prisoner slept, and a part of the room taken in. Well, next day he saw only five windows ; the day following showed him but four ; then three, then two, then one, the room gradually growing smaller. Imagine his agony ! He had now to crawl on his hands and knees, and that night the room closed in on itself and him, and he was crushed to death."

" Wal," said Hank, taking a fresh chew, " I'll guess the man who invented that thing must have lessons from Old Nick himself."

" It was very awful."

" And it is true ?"

" Oh, yes. In the Middle Ages men were very cruel. People were burnt at the stake, boiled in oil, and killed in all sorts of unpleasant ways."

" Bad as injuns !"

" Quite."

This story made Hank very thoughtful, and he hurried over his work.

When the party was loaded, he said—

" It'll take three more days to get the rest of this meat home ; but then we'll be stocked up for the winter, and as we don't know where we are going, or what we've got before us, it's as well to be independent of the butcher, and have your own meat-market to go to for a roast, more especially as the butcher don't take in this spot on his route."

They hurried home.

All were anxious to see if Mr. Mole would welcome them back.

Hank expected he would be all right, but Jack had his doubts, and Monday said—

" Mr. Mole gone coon, sure. Not likely to see um Professor any more."

" How so, Monday ?" asked Jack.

" Because the Witch Queen got him "

" The witch ?"

" In my country we believe in um witches sah," replied Monday. " If you good, and wear fetish charms, scare witch away."

" You surely are not so ignorant and soft as to think that ?"

" That's so, Mast Jack. Um witch got um soft thing in Mist Mole. He get full as um goat on whisky, and she scoop um in."

" Rubbish !"

" Bet you ten pounds, sah."

Jack made no reply, and they quickened their movements, soon afterwards reaching the camp.

The white tents, rendered all the more ghastly by the surrounding of snow, stood out clearly in the foreground.

" Toot yer horn, squire," said Hank.

"Yes; he and his friends are at the Gap, but although I tried to get him killed, the luck was against me. However, I know he's on this island, and we'll go for him again, sure, when the weather breaks."

"Yes, yes !"

It had been arranged between Fannie and her husband that he should say nothing about her having been disguised as an Indian, as Olalla might not have liked her if he had known that she was the original Ghost-that-Lies-in-the-Wood.

Red-Dog and Blue-Horse were bad enough in his eyes: but he hated Ghost-that-Lies-in-the-Wood worse than all.

Olalla asked a quantity of questions about Flyaway Gap and Harkaway, which Hunston answered briefly, saying he would talk more fully after supper.

He led Fannie to the log-houses.

"This is your home for the present," he exclaimed, pointing to the one he occupied.

"It is good enough," she exclaimed.

Viola was close by.

"Mrs. Harkaway," he cried.

She looked at him with tear-stained eyes, which denoted she had been weeping.

"Yes," she exclaimed.

"This lady is my wife," he continued.

"Surely I have seen her somewhere before," said Viola.

"Perhaps you have, and perhaps you haven't. That does not matter any one way or the other."

"Certainly not."

"You and your son," said Hunston, "will in future wait upon my wife. In fact, you will be her servants, and she will have my perfect permission to punish any disobedience or inattention in any way she thinks fit, just as if you were slaves on a Cuban plantation."

"I shan't wait on anyone," answered young Jack, defiantly.

"You won't, eh !"

"No, sir; and you can't make me. What's more, I'm not going to allow mamma to be any woman's slave."

"Hush! my dear boy," said Viola. "We are in the power of those bad men, and we cannot help ourselves. We must do as they tell us."

"Will you wait on that woman?"

"I will do all they ask me in reason."

"No you shan't," replied Young Jack.

Fannie beckoned to the boy.

"Go and bring me some drinking-water!" she exclaimed.

"Go and get it yourself," replied Young Jack.

He sat down on a log and looked boldly at her.

"Do you allow me to be defied ? " she said, appealing to Hunston.

"Certainly not. He is an unlicked cub, and we must teach him better manners," he replied.

He beckoned to the two Indians and to Pete.

"Take that boy, Pete, and bind him fast to one of those saplings by the water's edge."

"Yes, sah," replied the negro.

He approached Young Jack.

"You hear what Marse Hunston say, sah," he exclaimed. "But come 'long quietly, and not have a fuss."

"I shan't move of my own free will," answered the boy, doggedly.

"Have to move you, shuah."

"Is it right that mamma and I should be detail'd to wait on a red headed girl like that?"

beautiful golden hair was red. The idea ! Would you let him call the tresses you love red, dear ?"

"No," replied Hunston, biting his lips. "He's a durned sight too cheeky. Pete !"

"What dat, Marse Hunston ?"

"Do as I tell you, or I'll give you such a cutting up as you have not had since you left your plantation."

"Hole on now, sah. Don't give dis chile no cuttin' up. He's good boy, and don't require it. Dat sort of lickin' got old-fashioned, and gone out with de war, shuah."

He was alarmed at Hunston's threat, and seized Young Jack by the arm to drag him to the nearest sapling, having already provided himself with a coil of rope.

Jack resisted, and kicked Pete in his struggle to release himself.

"Oh ! de good Lord. Dat sort of kickin' not agree with my anatomy. Come 'long, you vicious young cuss. You'll make dis nigger swar soon, wuss dan a Michigan farmer's wife when de farmer's cow kicks over de milk-pail. Bless de Lord ! Dere it is again. What you think dis chile made of, any way ? Now stop dat kicking, Marse Jack."

With some difficulty, he got the boy to the tree, when the Indians helped to bind him.

Pete sat down rubbing his shins, and lamenting over "de sufferin' dere is in dis world."

Hunston had been engaged in cutting a long, lithe switch from a tree, which he handed to Fannie.

"Go and beat him yourself," he said.

"Just what I should like to do," she replied. "Only I fear I couldn't hurt him enough."

This speech revealed the viciousness of her nature, and showed how much of the tigress there was beneath the surface.

"Lay it on," answered Hunston. "You'll make him squeal, I know."

"It shan't be my fault if I don't," she rejoined. "I'll teach him to refuse to obey me, and tell me I have red hair. It's like his impudence."

She advanced to the boy, and began to strike him over the back with the switch.

He turned his head round and laughed at her.

"Is that all you can do?" he said, tauntingly.

"If I can't hurt you, I'll get one of the Indians to do it for me," she replied.

Viola had looked on for some time, and she saw that, in spite of the boy's bravado, he was suffering acutely, as the tears had come into his eyes, though he was too brave to cry out.

Rushing forward she seized the stick, dragged it out of Fannie's hand, and broke it in half.

"Ha !" cried Fannie. "Do you want whipping, too ?"

"Are you a woman or a fiend ?" said Viola.

"A fiend to you and yours, Mrs. Harkaway."

"What harm have I ever done you ? " asked Viola, in surprise.

"It is your husband who has wronged me."

"My husband ?"

"Yes. He told me he loved me, and then rejected me."

This was not true, but the shaft went home.

All Viola's fiery, jealous nature was aroused, for she saw that Fanny was pretty, and thought there might be some foundation for her story.

"My husband loved you ? I'll not believe it," she said, unwilling to let Fannie see she was when I have taught you to be civil and obedient, I will set you both all the menial tasks I can find, and make you feel the bitterness of your servitude."

She waved her hand to Hunston.

He came up.

"Tie Mrs. Harkaway," she said, "and let one Indian whip the boy while the other beats the woman. I will tell them when to stop."

Her commands were quickly executed.

Two Indians went after the unfortunate woman, who had turned away, scornfully, from the beautiful fiend.

Viola was arrested by a tall Indian, in her mournful meditations, and dragged away to be flogged at a tree.

She did not resist; she knew it would be useless. Casting a despairing look at Young Jack, she suffered herself to be bound to a tree.

The Indians commenced the punishment, and not till Viola had fainted under the severity of the discipline, and Young Jack's jacket was torn into threads, and his back torn and blistered, did she order them to stop.

"Untie them, and let them go," she said.

Young Jack bent over the insensible form of Viola, while Fannie, perfectly content, retired to her hut with Hunston.

Olalla smiled grimly.

Viola did not open her eyes, nor did she make any response to the boy's address.

She had fainted.

He grew alarmed.

More, he grew indignant.

"They have killed her," he muttered.

For a moment he hesitated.

Then he ran to the hut occupied by Hunston and his bride.

"Come out," he cried, knocking at the rude door. "Come out, you overgrown coward! I want to speak to you."

The door opened, and Hunston appeared on the threshold.

Behind him was his wife, the beautiful Fanny.

"What do you want?" asked Hunston. "Can't I enjoy an hour's quiet without being interrupted by you?"

"No," replied Jack.

"Haven't you had enough, eh, for one day?"

"I've strength enough left to give you something?"

Saying this, Young Jack stood upon his toes, and dealt Hunston a blow in the face which cut his lip and made it bleed.

"By Jove!" cried Hunston, spitting out the blood. "This is too much."

"Come in." said Fanny. "Let him be."

"I will not."

"He is only a boy, and we will punish him again presently."

Hunston drew a pistol.

"I'll shoot him!" he cried.

Young Jack made a grab at the pistol, resolved to sell his life dearly, and a struggle ensued for the possession of the weapon.

Fiercely they fought for it.

They writhed and twisted, but Hunston had superior strength, and the crisis of the contest did not appear doubtful.

Suddenly the pistol exploded.

The muzzle was turned in the direction of Fannie, and the bullet lodged in her breast.

hole in her breast, and she was breathing with difficulty.

"Are you hurt, dearest?" he asked

"Oh, yes," she replied.

"Not much, my darling. Say not much."

"I am dying"

Hunston gnashed his teeth with rage

Young Jack stood appalled for a moment at the catastrophe of which he was the innocent cause.

In struggling with Hunston he had only endeavoured to save his own life.

It did not enter his imagination for a moment to kill anybody.

Least of all, Fannie.

Certainly, he was irritated against her, and Hunston, too, on account of their cruelty to him and Viola, but he did not hunger for the lives of either of them.

Olalla and the Indians had gone on the lake to look for some fish, having, Indian-fashion, set some lines in holes they had made in the ice.

They were some distance off

If they heard the report of the shot, they did not pay any attention to it.

The only spectator of the tragedy was Pete.

With a shrewdness which did him infinite credit, he saw that young Jack stood in great danger.

Fannie was evidently wounded to the death.

Hunston would be infuriated, and probably sacrifice the boy to his resentment as soon as he realised the fact of his wife's speedy death.

The only hope of salvation was in flight.

Hunston was kneeling on the frozen ground by Fannie's side, trying to stanch the blood which flowed from the gaping wound.

His efforts were in vain

Her life was ebbing fast.

"Dear, dear Fannie!" he cried. "Don't leave me just when I have learnt to love you fondly."

"I am dying," she gasped, painfully.

"Oh! that cursed boy; but I will have blood for blood."

"Don't leave me."

"No, no. What can I do?"

"Nothing."

"Is there no hope?"

"None this side of the grave; pray for me. I have blood on my soul."

"I—I don't know how to pray," replied Hunston, hesitatingly.

"Pray, pray."

He raised his haggard face to the dull sky of heaven, and murmured in his agony—

"Oh! God, spare her life. Do not take her from me!"

"That—is—a selfish prayer," Fannie said. "Pray for me"

Again he lifted up his voice.

"Oh! God in heaven, have mercy on her dying soul!"

"That is better. Thank you, dearest."

A serene smile of satisfaction flitted over her features.

Then her eyes glazed in the rigidity of death.

She was dying now.

Young Jack looked on with painful emotions.

He had no reason to care for this woman; indeed if he had known the persecution to which she had subjected his father he would have hated her.

"Then where has she gone to?"

"That is the mystery."

"I'd give a thousand pounds for just one glimpse of light on this thing."

"So would I."

"What is your opinion, Hank?" said Harvey.

"It isn't Indians, squire," replied Hank, "and it isn't white men. It's jest one of these things that you can't give an opinion about. Let's set a watch, so's we aren't gobbled up, and wait till daybreak."

There was nothing else to be done, and the watch having been appointed, sleep soon fell upon the camp.

Harvey was restless.

Hilda had been a good, kind, loving, affectionate wife to him, and her loss was the severest blow which Heaven could have dealt him.

He puzzled his brain during the silent watches of that long, dark, dismal night, in trying to think how she had disappeared.

The mystery was so deep and maddening that it was as bewildering as trying to think of the end of space, the limit of the universe.

He gave it up in despair.

She was lost to him.

Would he ever see her again, hear her cheery voice and see the flash of her dark, liquid eye?

He asked himself the question, and the wind moaning over the snow-clad waste, seemed to answer, Never; and then he succumbed to exhausted nature and slept.

Just at that silent hour—the transition of night to day—Jack Harkaway was suddenly awakened by the fierce growling of a strange dog, which was standing over him with its fore-paws upon his shoulders.

Always on the alert, Jack started up, and as he did so he saw the shadow of a man fall upon the trunk of a tree and instantly disappear. Starting to his feet, Harkaway seized his gun and made a search for the substance of the shadow, but there were no signs of any living beings besides his companions to be seen.

Thinking that the shadow was a creation of his troubled mind, he threw himself down again to snatch what rest he could, but the incident troubled him greatly, and kept him awake.

There was something more in it than he could make out. The dog, too, coming as it did at such a time, seemed like an interposition of Providence to shield him from the unknown danger which menaced him. Where had the animal come from? and to whom could it belong?

These questions were unanswerable, and Jack was more puzzled when he looked round and found the dog had gone.

He determined not to mention anything of what had occurred to his companions, but to try and fathom the mystery by himself.

When day broke, Harvey was the first to go and explore the chasm which Mr. Mole had pronounced a crater of an extinct volcano, and there was little doubt, from its appearance and general formation, that his opinion was correct.

The sides were jagged and precipitous.

It seemed possible for a man or a boy to climb up or go down the side, using the projecting ledges as stepping-stones; but how far would he have to go, and whither would it lead the explorer?

That was the question.

The snow had been swept away so as to make a path to the water, and consequently, if Hilda had gone in that direction, they could not trace her by her footsteps.

There was not even a handkerchief or a piece of a dress to indicate whether she had been there or not.

Harvey looked dismally down the yawning gulf.

He was roused from his reverie by Jack, who touched him on the shoulder.

"See here!" he exclaimed, exhibiting a coil of rope with a big heavy stone attached to the end.

"What's that for?" inquired Harvey.

"To try the depth of this hole. I'd like to know if we could fathom it."

Carefully he lowered the stone and ran out about four hundred and fifty yards of rope, without touching the bottom.

"No go!" he exclaimed. "I've payed out a quarter of a mile of rope, and can't touch the bottom."

"Then there is very little hope for Hilda," sighed Harvey.

"Do you think she has tumbled down the pit?"

"I do. What else could have become of her?"

"Heaven only knows. It's a terrible mystery."

CHAPTER XV.
MORE MYSTERIOUS DISAPPEARANCES.

JACK HARKAWAY would have comforted Harvey if he could have done so, but there was so little room for hope, that he did not consider himself justified in holding out any.

"Will you come along with us to-day?" he asked.

"Where are you going to?"

"After the rest of the bear-meat. Hank says he means to have it all, and the cubs, too, and it will take us nearly a week to get it stowed away in camp."

"I'll go if you can't do without me. Never shirk duty. That would not do," said Harvey.

"If you'd rather stay here, Dick——"

"I would."

"All right. Then we will dispense with your services."

"I might hear or see something," answered Harvey, "which will give me some clue to Hilda's fate!"

"I hope you may. Keep your eyes open and your rifle cocked. There may be some deeper mystery about this than we imagine at present," remarked Jack.

"No fear. I'll not go to sleep."

There was a bitter wind blowing down the cold sides of the snow-clad hills, and roaring over the undulating ground in front of them.

Jack shook Harvey by the hand, and looked kindly and affectionately into his eyes.

His look was more eloquent than words.

He felt that Jack pitied him, and in deep misfortune it is well to have the sympathy of our friends.

When Jack rejoined Hank, the latter jerked his thumb in Harvey's direction.

"Goin' to stay here and watch?" he said.

"Yes," said Jack, laconically.

"That's good. Now, we'll start after the b'ar meat. We mayn't have sich another chance in a good while."

"Am I to go, too?" asked Mr. Mole

"Why, certainly. We can't afford to leave a mule like you at home, eating his head off in the stable."

"Thank you for the comparison," said the Professor. "It is a piece of your usual politeness; but talking of beasts of burden, why not hitch up some of our mules to draw home the meat?"

"Kase they couldn't make no headway in the snow."

make some money, come up to the Harkaway settlement to-morrow afternoon, and ask for Mrs. Cabucaon."

"Who is she?"

"You will find out in due time; ask no more questions. Will you do it?"

"Dartazzan, I guess, ain't more particular than his neighbours, and if you want anyone laid out, plant down the stamps, and I'm willing."

"Is your name Dartazzan?"

"It is."

"Very well. I shall expect you to-morrow, Mr. Dartazzan," said Fannie, and she tripped away over the sandy shore, leaving the hunter much perplexed.

"She'll expect me," he muttered, "and I was to ask for Mrs. Cabuchon. How can she be a red Indian chief in the skin? There's something more in this than meets the eye; but I'll go."

Dartazzan did not attempt to bury Joe.

He sauntered leisurely along toward the Gap, thinking he would startle the boys with the news of Joe's death.

Dartazzan was not a working miner.

He was one of the loafers of St. Louis, who had started for the Black Hills at the commencement of the excitement about that region, expecting to pick up gold by pailfuls, and when he found that it was difficult to get a bare living by hard work, he did as little of it as he could, and was ready at a moment's notice, like Joe and Gosh, and many others at the Gap, to perpetrate any villainy to get the means of living in idleness.

On Jack's return home he did not hesitate to tell his friends what had happened.

Harvey was astonished.

"It's queer how Hunston could have found us out."

"Yes," said Hank, "and yer can bet yer boots that where that skunk is, Olalla's not far off.

"I'm sorry," remarked Mr. Mole, "that the Indians have gone away; they certainly were a protection."

"Fancy Ghost-that-lies-in-the-Wood being a woman, and that woman Mrs. Cabuchon, of all others!" observed Hilda. "But I must be charitable to her, and do all I can for her."

"I knew it all along," said Mole. "You cant fool me."

"You didn't know, it sir," said Harvey.

"That's right. Call me a liar," said Mole.

"I didn't mean that."

"You contradicted me flatly to my face. What is that but giving a man the lie direct? I can't tell what the young men of the present day are coming to," said the Professor.

"Well, if you did know, you kept it mighty dark."

"Of course I did: I had my reasons."

No one believed this assertion of Mole's, but he flattered himself he had made an impression, and was satisfied.

Toward evening an elegantly-attired lady came to the settlement.

She had beautiful golden hair, and her pretty, dimpled face was wreathed in smiles and blushes.

Hilda ran to meet her.

"You are Mrs. Cabuchon," she said. "Jack has told us all, and you must permit me to congratulate you upon being released from a

to deceive people. Did I make a very good Indian."

"Excellent."

"If I thought I was clever enough, I would adopt the stage as a profession."

"You would succeed. I am sure of it. Come into my house and take tea."

"Thanks," replied Fannie; "I would prefer to be alone in my own little hut."

"Well, if there is anything I can do for you, dear, let me know."

"I will not fail," replied Mrs Cabuchon.

Then Fannie kissed Hilda, and Hilda kissed Fannie, in the manner of women when they feel very good and friendly to one another.

But Fannie declined to be interviewed, or receive any company, and for the rest of the day she kept herself secluded in the privacy of her own log-hut.

The next day Hilda visited her, and the two women were very busy with needles and thread till dinner-time, as Mrs. Cabuchon's wardrobe had to be put in order.

All the morning Harkaway and Hank were in council together.

Hank recommended that an exploring party on a large scale should be organised, in order to accomplish two things.

The first was to look for the Mountain of Gold.

The second, to hunt down Hunston.

When the council was over, Lord Mossbunker and Hopkins were seen approaching.

They had been to the Gap.

"Good-bye!" exclaimed Lord Mossbunker.

"What's that for?" inquired Jack.

"We are going to—a—leave you," said his lordship "Fact is, I am tired of this life, and—sir—I have found a hotel."

"Didn't know there was such a thing hereabouts."

"Ah, you—a—don't know evewything my fwiend. Some time ago I—a—sent a message by the express to some bankers in Cheyenne. Had no money, you know, and wanted some. They—a—wote to my agents in New York, and the money has come to-day."

"Good for you," said Jack.

"I have 20,000 dollars. Not much for a man in—a—my position but enough to stay at the—a—shanty which they call a hotel till my eaws get well. Couldn't stay heaw, you know. Sort of thing no fellah could suffah long and live."

Hank heard this.

"Ain't yer an ongrateful old fossil?" he exclaimed.

"Eh?—a—what did you do me the honour to observe!" said Mossbunker, putting his glass in his eye.

"Ef yer ain't the ongratefulnest purpever I see raised by a kind owner I want ter know."

"Hopkins!" said Lord Mossbunker.

"Yes, m'lord."

"What are you standing there like a fool for?"

"Very sorry, m'lord."

"Very sorry? What's the use of that? Go and punch that man's head."

Hopkins shook his head.

"I'd rather decline, m'lord. He's too large and bugely for me."

"Wather decline! Well, perhaps you are right. We will part in—a—peace," said Lord Mossbunker. "Shall be glad to see you, Mr. Hark-

He could not tell.

With his heart throbbing wildly, he started on the homeward track.

"More of this devilish mystery?" he muttered.

He was right.

When he came back to camp Hank Smith was gone!

Jack had not been away more than half an hour, but the wolf had swept down on the fold.

In this case there was no sign of a struggle, and if Hank had been swallowed up by an earthquake, he could not have disappeared more completely.

The perspiration broke out all over Harkaway's frame.

It collected in beads on his forehead, and he leant on his rifle as he wiped his clammy brow.

"Good Heavens!" he exclaimed. "In the whole course of my adventurous career I never met with anything like this. First of all, Hilda went, then Harvey, after him, Mole, then Monday, then Hank, and——"

He broke off abruptly.

Something like mocking laughter seemed to come out of the gaping mouth of the extinct volcano.

He rushed to the brink.

Peered into its murky depths, but could see nor hear nothing.

"Only the wind," he muttered. "I am getting nervous, and enough to made me. Shall I be the victim of the unseen? What will be my fate? By Heaven, I'll have a fight for life!"

He sat down, and, taking out his pocket-flask, imbibed a draught of whisky.

It was well he did so.

He was trembling all over like a leaf, and his face had grown white as a sheet.

It was an awful position for him to be placed in.

He was alone in the wilderness of snow, in the depth of winter, all his friends gone he knew not where, he know not how, and a terrible mystery was hanging over him.

If he could only see his danger, know its magnitude, and grasp it, he would not care.

Harvey was brave, so was Monday; Hank was cool and sagacious.

They were not men to be easily overcome.

With an aching heart and a throbbing brow, Jack piled fresh pine-knots on the fire, and prepared his supper in the midst of a solemn silence, oppressive as the grave, and a vast, untrodden solitude, which might have struck terror into any one.

Wearily he waited for the shades of night to fall.

Going into his tent, he wrapped himself up in skins and blankets to keep out the intense cold, and, with one hand on his rifle, the other on a pistol, he went off into a fitful slumber

What would that night bring forth?

He dared not think of it.

Exhausted nature required repose, and he had to sleep, though he would gladly have watched all night.

In the daytime he would not have cared, because, with all his faculties about him, he would stand a better chance if attacked.

His dreams were of the most frightful and hideous character.

Now he was fighting with an army of demons, breathing fire and smoke, and who were trying to drag him down to the bottomless pit.

he was bound to a tree, unable to resist them.

Towards midnight he awoke.

Getting up, he looked out of the tent

The silvery moon cast its pale rays on the earth, and made the snow sparkle beneath its beams.

But the camp was deserted.

No enemy had entered it while he slept.

Jack Harkaway was alone.

The unknown terror would not, apparently, come in the night-time, and he had to battle against it some other time.

Having slept off his fatigue, he lighted his pipe and remained on the watch.

CHAPTER XVI.

MRS. HUNSTON AT HOME.

IT took Hunston and his wife six days to sail round the island to the point where Olalla was staying.

Once they were blown out into the bosom of the lake; but the wind changed, and Hunston regained his old course, coasting the island for the remainder of the distance.

They were very fortunate in having open weather.

The very day after their arrival, the severe weather which had overtaken Harkaway and his friends in the hills set in, and in one night the lake was frozen over several inches thick.

Hunston soon grew very fond of Fannie.

She was undeniably pretty, and her ways were very fascinating.

His constant attention pleased her.

She had never loved her former husband, Cabuobon.

He was too old, eccentric, hard, and severe a man to be loved.

But Hunston was young, and though the marriage, at first, was merely one of convenience—that is to say, for the purpose of hunting down Harkaway, they soon became attached to one another.

It was much nicer to be a young man's darling than an old man's slave, as she had been.

When they arrived at camp Olalla, the Indian chief, welcomed them with delight.

"Ugh!" he exclaimed. "Do me heap good to see you back, Hunston.'

"Thank you."

"What you done?"

"Tried to do a great deal, but it didn't all come off."

"See Harkaway?"

Hunston looked round.

Viola and Young Jack were standing together, regarding Fannie with some surprise.

But they were too far away to hear anything.

The two Indians—all that now remained of Olalla's once powerful band of Crows and Bannocks—were piling logs o a fire as quickly as Pete, the negro, could cut them.

"First of all," said Hunston, "allow me to introduce my wife."

"You got squaw?

"Yes."

Olalla elevated his eyebrows in surprise.

"Pretty girl. Much handsome," he said. "Where you find her?"

"Flyaway Gap."

"What sort of place that?"

"Quite a colony of miners!"

"You find him there?"

"I did.'

"Good! See Harkaway?"

made his fortune in a single day.

"Here, my man, it you want to earn a few dollars, I'll tell you how to do it."

"Orright, Sammy's no objection," replied the idiot, grinning as he spoke.

"Go up to the Gap and borrow a large wickerwork basket and a wheelbarrow. Put the basket on the barrow and wheel it down to me. If any one asks you what you a e doing or interferes with you, say Tom Wanzer sent you. Do you understand?"

The fellow grinned in a more diabolical manner than before, but did not offer to move.

"Do you hear when you're spoken to?" vociferated Hunston.

"I hear yer fast enough. But Sammy dearly loves gold, and he is not going to leave what he's found. Sammy's found bags of gold, and he means to keep them."

"You crazy fool!" cried Hunston, springing out of the trench he had been digging. "The treasure is mine. I found it."

"And so did I find it. Give me half. Give poor Sammy half, and he will fetch the barrow."

"I won't give you a bit; but I'll tell you what I'll give you—a sound hiding."

Hunston stood on tiptoe and broke down a branch, which he stripped of leaves and superfluous twigs.

He advanced toward Slinking Sammy, and holding it up threateningly, said:—

"Now, you see this? Well, if you don't do as I tell you, it will soon make acquaintance with your shoulders, in a manner more forcible than pleasant. Don't make any mistake about me when my blood is up!"

The half-witted fellow winced a little at this threat, but appeared to be more enamoured of the treasure than before.

He threw himself upon it, and, stretching out his arms, embraced it lovingly, hugging the bags to his breast, and saying, in a whining voice—

"Sammy's! all Sammy's!"

"We'll soon see how much of it is Sammy's!" exclaimed Hunston, with a coarse laugh. "Come here, my fine fellow. You'd better come, or I'll have to come and fetch you. Oh, you won't, eh? Mean to be obstinate, do you? Very well; all the worse for you. I used to be a good hand for laying it on, and I'll try if I can welt you to your satisfaction."

A couple of lengthy strides brought him to the idiot.

He grovelled and wriggled at his feet, looking up in his face, as if deprecating the threatened violence, but still clinging to the gold, as if his whole soul was wrapt up in it, and to lose it would be worse than death itself.

Hunston caught hold of him by the collar of his ragged coat and shook him as a terrier dog does a rat.

Slinking Sammy did not appear to think him in earnest, for he laughed and gibbered, and contorted his features, and grimaced like a monkey, saying—

"All Sammy's. No more rags. No more eating cheese-rinds and old crusts. Sammy will live in a big place and have servants to wait upon him, and he'll drink wine, and eat venison and turtle. Sammy's in luck. Mother always told Sammy that he would be fortunate some day, and she said true, for he's as rich as a king."

Hunston cut this soliloquy short by lifting up his switch and bringing it down with all his force upon the idiot's shoulders.

"Take that," he exclaimed, grating his teeth

that. How do you like your fortune, eh? Will you do what you're told the next time a gentleman speaks to you?"

Although the pain must have been great, Slinking Sammy did not cry aloud, as might have been expected.

He wriggled and writhed, as if he wished to escape from the thraldom in which he was held, but he did not roar, as Hunston anticipated he would

He uttered strange cries like the bark of a dog, or the subdued yelp of a hound around whose flanks the sting of the lash of the whipper-in still lingers.

"Let me go!" cried Slinking Sammy. "I'll do it. I'll do anything; but we musn't make a noise, or someone will come and rob us of our treasure. I'll fetch the barrow and—what else was it?—the hamper. I'll bring them both. Don't whip me any more. Let poor Sammy alone; he never did you any harm."

Hunston was satisfied with his promise; he threw his switch down, relinquished his hold of the idiot, and sat down upon the bags of gold.

Unfortunately for himself, he did not glance at Slinking Sammy's countenance, or he would have read therein a terrible vow of revenge.

His face was convulsed with rage and passion. It was full of malignancy, and foreboded something antagonistic to Hunston's welfare.

The eyes positively glared like those of an angry serpent.

The corners of the mouth were drawn down, and twitched convulsively.

The command which he had over his features, however, was very remarkable, for no sooner was Hunston's hand raised than the passion faded away in the same instantaneous manner in which it had arisen, and he was once more the prowling, slinking idiot, without one idea to call his own.

"Now, be off with you!" exclaimed Hunston. "Bring that basket and that barrow; and if you are long over your job, I pity you. Mind you this, too, young fellow, don't utter a word to any mortal soul about gold or anything else. If you do, you'll catch it for that, you may take my word. Say, if you are spoken to, that you are sent by Wanzer—that's enough. Everyone will be satisfied with that. Do you understand, or shall I tell you again?"

"No, no; Sammy understands."

Hunston advised him to run the whole way, if he wished to preserve an entire skin.

The idiot set off at a swift pace, and was soon out of sight.

"Doosed awkward, that half-witted thief coming upon me just when he wasn't wanted," muttered Hunston, as soon as he was alone. "I'd ever so much rather have seen a ghost; but it don't much matter. I'll make a beast of burden of him. It's all he's fit for. He shall wheel the barrow of gold to the boat for me. How far is the lake shore from here? A good fifteen miles. Never mind, we can do it in five hours, easy—oh! in less than that. I'll make the fellow run. Never fear but what I'll take it out of him.

As he sat on his bags of gold in the ruins of that old hut, his mind soared up into the highest regions of romance.

His delicious reveries were disturbed by the return of the idiot, who had brought the hamper and the barrow with him.

"So you're back at last. You'd be a nice fellow to send for sorrow, I must say."

"Why is that?"

"Because you would be so long fetching it."

pil d up in great rampart-like banks all round the camp.

A pathway was kept open to the "ash-pit," down which, as we have said, all refuse was thrown.

A mule died of cold, and he was cast down the crater of the extinct volcano.

Hank busied himself in making snow-shoes for the party.

He was in high spirits.

In twenty-four hours the snow was over, but it was bitterly cold.

The depth of the snow was over a foot.

When the snow-shoes were made, the old hunter proposed a search for bears.

"I tell you, fellows," he said, "that b'ars' meat's good, and can't be beat. We've eat it before, and we're goin' so eat it agin."

Hinda was to remain in camp.

Mr. Mole shouldered his rifle, as did Jack, Harvey, and Monday, and, under the experienced guidanceship of Hank, they started early in the morning.

A trudge through the snow of about six miles brought them to the edge of a pine wood.

The tall funereal-looking trees were heavily laden with the white mantle which had fallen on them

But Hank did not look at the trees.

He was prospecting for tracks.

At last he found them.

"Look a-here, kernel," he exclaimed, pointing to certain marks in the snow; "we've struck 'em good!"

"Yes," replied Jack; "that's a bear."

"And nothing else?"

"What besides?"

"She's got two cubs, and don't you forget it. Cubs is splendid eatin', and we've got ter hev them."

"Good enough, Hank," replied Jack. "Let's follow them up."

"They've got a cave somewhere near," said Hank. "Foller me, fellers, and yer can all get in yer lead soon's yer see the varmint."

"That will just suit me," said Mole. "I have killed thousands of bears in my time, and——"

"What air ye givin' me now?" asked Hank, interrupting him with a disdainful air.

"The truth."

"I'll bet yer never killed a bar yet. Oh! yes yer did; I mind me now; but it was by accident. Yer hid in a holler tree, and a hive of bees drew yer out to fight."

"Oh! you can make as much fun of me as you like," replied the Professor. "I'll lead this party, and you shall see whether any quantity of bears can scare me."

"You won't get frightened, not a little bit, until yer see 'em," replied Hank.

Mr. Mole could not make any further reply.

He put on his spectacles, fastened his gaze on the tracks which were plainly visible in the snow, and started ahead.

"Let anyone follow me who likes!" he exclaimed. "I'm resolved on killing bears to-day."

The rest of the party went after him, and the bear-tracks led towards the forest of pines.

It was probable that the bears lived in some hollow or cave thereabouts.

Suddenly the Professor, after going about half a mile with his head bent forward, like a dog on the scent, fell heavily forward.

He had put his foot in a hole.

Off rolled his spectacles, his rifle fell from his grasp, and he knocked his mouth badly against a piece of rock which protruded above the snow.

Jack picked him up and set him on his feet.

"Are you hurt, sir?" he asked.

"Yum, yum!" replied the Professor.

"Swallowed a tooth, sir?"

"Um!"

Jack slapped him vigorously on the back, and a little colour came back into the Professor's face.

He drew his breath and gasped.

"What's got yer, anyway, Professor?" asked Hank.

"Um!"

"Can't yer speak?"

"Num, num!"

"Blessed if I don't think the old fool's swallered a chew of tobaccer," said Hank. "I lent him half a pauer afore we started, and I seed him put a big plug in his mouth not over a quarter of an hour ago. Is that it, Professor?"

"Yum, yum!" said Mole.

"Ef yer don't speak, I'll knock the life out of yer."

"Num, num! Um! Yum, yum! Um!"

"Strike me silly! I'll settle this!" exclaimed Hank.

He raised his fist, and gave Mole a blow in the stomach, which doubled him up.

Then there as a slight gurgling noise, and Mole breathed again.

The colour came back into his face.

He gasped for breath, and was at last able to speak.

"Hank, your hand," he said.

"Shake, kernel," said the hunter.

"You have saved me from a great danger."

"I hev?"

"Yes. You were right in your surmise. I did swallow my chew, and I also swallowed a tooth, which I knocked out against that rock. But your vigorous attack upon my back has restored everything to its proper—a—proper—Jack, help me to a word. I am still somewhat confused."

"Equilibrium, sir," said Jack.

"That's good. Let it stand at that!" exclaimed Mole.

"Wal, squire," said Hank. "I'm glad you didn't come to much harm, 'cause ef yer was to lay up I'd hev no one to la'f at. But I've saved you from mor'n yer think."

"What?"

"B'ars."

"Nonsense!"

"Ef yer doubt my word," cried Hank, "go down in the hollow thar under that rock. The she b'ar's thar with the cubs. I'll bet yer."

"How do you know?"

"How do I know?" repeated the hunter, with a quiet chuckle. "What I don't know on b'ars ain't worth larning. I say they're in thar Yer gritty, go in and see."

"Thank you!" exclaimed Mole. "I appreciate your kindness, my friend, at its full value, but I'd rather decline the invitation just now."

"Wall, thar's the b'ar. Mrs. B'ar and all the little b'ar's, and p'r'aps Mr. B'ar. They invite you to a social, and you decline. Next——"

"I'll go down!" exclaimed Jack.

He was in a desperate sort of humour, and just in the frame of mind to tackle any danger.

Fearlessly Jack stepped down between the boulders.

It seemed as if there was a cave below, but the snowdrift was so thick that he could not be sure of anything.

"Wel, if snow come, it cover up tracks in ten minutes, and so might just as well start in the morning as now. Me want eat fish. Sleep good."

Hunston could not argue the point any longer.

He saw the force of Olalla's reasoning, and was forced to give way.

Nothing would be gained by an early start.

Still, his fiery nature made him pant for action.

He longed fiercely to avenge the death of the fair Fannie on Young Jack and Viola.

He could have cut them with a knife and bathed his hands in their blood.

"Oh!" he cried, gnashing his teeth, "I could dabble in their gore as if it was water on a July day!"

The Indians busied themselves in cooking the fish, of which Hunston partook sparingly.

That night was the most wretched he ever passed in his life.

He had to sleep in the same hut with the corpse of the woman he loved, and who had been his so short—ah! how short—a time!

It was intensely cold.

But so feverishly excited was his system, that he did not feel the inclemency of the weather.

The next day Olalla and Hunston started in pursuit of the fugitives.

Though snow had fallen all night, the day was clear, with a keen, frosty air.

Their object point was the chain of hills.

Olalla argued, with characteristic sagacity, that the runaways would make for the hills.

In their recesses they would find shelter and game.

Nor was he wrong.

After two days' weary and laboured travelling they reached the hills.

A huge, overhanging crag sheltered a spot of ground.

On this the wind had driven a very thin covering of snow.

"Ha!" ejaculated the chief of the Bannocks.

"What's up?" asked Hunston.

"See."

Olalla pointed to a mark in the snow.

It was a footprint.

Near it were others, and they were some of them of different sizes.

"Good," said Olalla. "Come on trail."

"How?"

"See little foot, woman. Bit bigger, boy. Great big foot, black man."

"By George, you're right."

"This luck," said Olalla. "Now we follow them right straight along and come up with them soon. Haven't gone back. Can't cross hills. Got in cave somewhere."

"I guess so," replied Hunston.

He was deeply gratified by this discovery.

It seemed as if his revenge was within his grasp.

He and the Indian carefully followed the tracks, which conducted them to the side of the hill.

Here there was a large fissure, which was the mouth of a cave.

"Ha!" cried Olalla, with another exclamation of surprise. "Come to Kehamas."

"What in the world are Kehamas?"

"Great caves. All under mountains. Heard Indians who been here many years ago speak of them."

"How many years?"

"Great number. 'Foreme born.'"

"Oh! You mean it is a tradition with your tribe?" said Hunston.

"Yes. Handed down. Father speak to son Sabe?"

"I do."

"In Kehamas in the Kesapa," continued Olalla, "they say live Pe-bo-a. Very old Indian woman. She keep caves. Live in charge of some treasure. Indians live in those hills once. Lightning and thunder drive them away, because they wicked, and the Great Spirit angry with them. Only Pe-bo-a remains to guard secrets of the tribe."

"Is this the legend?"

"It is."

They had now neared the entrance to the cavernous recesses.

Olalla stood irresolute.

A shudder ran through his frame.

"Not like to go any further," he said.

"Why?" demanded Hunston.

"Afraid of Pe-bo-a. It is death to enter the Kehamas."

"Bosh!"

"Always been told so. Getting dark, too."

"No doubt Young Jack, Mrs. Harkaway, and Pete have taken refuge in the cave. Why should not we?"

"Get killed. Best stay here."

"Killed? Who by? The old woman?" said Hunston, with a scornful laugh.

"Yes. Pe-bo-a kill."

"Well, if you're fool enough to believe that, I am not. Why, I thought you were above that stupid rubbish, Olalla?"

"My brother does not know everything."

"If you won't come I'll go alone."

"Stop here. Make fire. Eat, sleep. See to-morrow."

CHAPTER XVII.

THE LAST OF THE BANNOCKS.

"THAT be darned for a yarn, I'm going in right away. If you're coward enough to leave——"

"Olalla no coward."

The chief drew himself up proudly.

"Come on, then."

"Olalla not got anything to live for now. All his young men are dead—fallen like leaves before the arm of Har-ka-wa. He will go into the Kehamas with his brother. Where a white man will go a red man knows no fear."

"That's plucky."

"Olalla has spoken! Is it good?"

"I admire you for that," said Hunston. "Let's get a stock of pine-knots and sail in."

The sides of the hill were covered with pine-trees, and with the aid of the Indian's tomahawk they collected a quantity of the highly resinous knots to light them on their journey through the caves.

By rubbing two sticks together with great industry for a long while Olalla got a light.

He informed Hunston that the Kehamas were said to be of great size, enormous length, and remarkable for their beauty.

But as he had never known anyone who had seen them, he could not vouch for the truth of this report.

When all was ready, the two men, grasping their rifles firmly with one hand, and the pine-knots, which blazed brightly, in the other, entered the gloomy recesses.

Soon they disappeared within the mysterious depth of the weird-looking Kehamas, and were

"Thank you, Hilda," he said. "I want it."

"Let me go and fetch Mrs Cabuchon. She will be as pleased as any of us to hear of your return!" continued Hilda.

"Stop!" cried Jack.

"Why?"

"I want you to hear what has happened to me, and then you can judge whether you ought to send for Mrs. Cabuchon or not."

Hilda looked surprised.

"I ain't got more'n three stools in my shanty," said Hank, "but you three can take 'em, and Monday and I will sit on what nature's given us."

He suited the action to the word, and sat down on the ground, Monday placing himself by his side.

Jack circumstantially related all that had occurred since his disappearance, concluding with the death of Dartazzan and the scene in the saloon.

Every one was astonished.

"I wouldn't have thought it of her," said Hilda.

"I would," said Hank. "Didn't I allus say as Ghost was a bad lot?"

"You did," replied Jack.

"I don't like to be hard on a woman," said Harvey, "but it is my opinion that she deserves to die."

"I say nothing at present," said Jack. "But I want the opinion of the whole. Harvey has declared his without being asked."

"I am with him," said Hank.

"And you, Hilda?"

"Death is very horrible," she answered.

"She did not think so when she gave me up to Redlynch and Dartazzan."

"That's so. What she meted out to you she deserves to suffer herself."

"What do you say, friend Monday?"

"Cut um throat, sah."

"I give the casting vote for her death, and that settles it," said Jack.

At this, Hilda's womanly nature revolted against the sentence.

"She is so young," she said.

"And so wicked," said Harvey.

"She is so pretty and winning in her manners, in spite of her—her red hair."

"Auburn locks make no difference, if the soul is black," said Harvey.

Jack had, as we know, a stern sense of justice, though he was as much inclined to be merciful as any man.

"I don't care about this woman hunting me down any more," he said, "and I want it stopped. Hunston is as much as I can tackle just now. You have all said she deserves to die. I look upon you as judge and jury. Do I understand you to have pronounced sentence of death upon her?"

"Yes," replied Harvey, slowly.

"Yes," said Hank, gravely.

"That's me," said Monday, "I'm solid on that."

Jack looked inquiringly at Hilda.

She did not speak.

"Silence gives consent with a woman," he exclaimed; "the verdict is unanimous. Fannie Cabuchon must die. She has attempted my life, and will do so again if she is allowed the chance. I must protect myself; there is no organised court in this wild place, and we have to be our own police, judges, and executioners. Monday!"

"Sah!"

"You have a pistol?"

Then Monday grinned, and showed his weapon.

"You have heard the sentence of this court," exclaimed Jack, "and I appoint you executioner,"

"What um do, sah?"

"Carry out the sentence of the court."

Monday was about to depart on his mission, when Hilda exclaimed, "Stop!"

"You speak to me, Missy Hilda?" said Monday.

"I did."

She advanced her stool to Harkaway, and said :—

"Give her until to-morrow morning. Will you not?"

"No!" exclaimed Jack.

"I have learnt to like her lately, and I should wish to comfort her in her last moments. Can you refuse me this request?"

"I must."

"Have I not already been your friend?"

"Always."

"And Dick, has he not——"

"Don't say a word about that," interrupted Jack. "Dick and I have already been like brothers."

Jack was silent.

He seemed to be arguing a point with himself.

Suddenly he rose, and took Hilda by the hand.

"I can refuse you nothing," he exclaimed.

"Thank you," she replied.

"Is it her life you ask?"

"I am not sure—I——" stammered Hilda. Then she stopped short.

"You intended to warn her of her peril, and let her go in the darkness of the night. Was it not?"

"I admit it."

"Well, her life was justly forfeited, but you have asked for it, and, as I have said before, I can refuse you nothing."

"Surely you are not afraid of a woman?"

"But such a vindictive woman! She is capable of doing and daring all things!"

"She shall trouble you no more."

"How?"

"I will make her promise, on her sacred word of honour, that she will molest you no more," said Hilda.

"Will she not laugh at promises?" replied Jack, doubtfully.

"Oh, oh! There is no woman so bad but what she has some good in her, away down in her heart."

"Go!" said Jack. "She is yours to do what you like with. You have saved her."

Hilda smiled.

"But," added Jack, with the old stony look coming over his face once more, "if she is found around here any more she will be shot."

"I understand."

Hilda tripped away, and sought Fannie, who was seated in her hut, reading a book by the light of a kerosene-lamp.

"Mrs. Cabuchon!" she exclaimed, "I have come to save you."

"From what?" anxiously asked Fannie.

"Death!"

"What have I done, and who threatens me?"

"Jack has escaped, after killing Redlynch and Dartazzan."

"Heaven help me!" cried Fannie.

"You must help yourself. Your death was decided on a few minutes ago. I begged you off but you must fly at once."

"Where can I go?"

Jack wound the horn, and made a cheery "Tra-lara-lara-lara—tra-la-la-la."

But, as on the preceding night, there was no reply.

"By thunder!" said Hank, "they've scooped the Professor."

"It looks like it," answered Jack.

Skimming over the frozen surface of the snow, they entered camp and hunted for Mr. Mole.

He was nowhere to be seen.

A rifle, a pistol, and an empty flask lying on the ground told a tale.

He had been there, armed and ready for the fray, but the unseen enemy had conquered him.

No trace whatever remained of him.

Jack's heart beat quickly, and he pressed his hand to his throbbing brow.

"There is some infernal mystery about this," he exclaimed, "which I must and will solve. We will all stay home to-morrow."

"That's what's the matter," replied Hank.

"If the raid is continued, we shall at least know what agency is at work, and have the satisfaction of fighting for our lives."

"Yer head's clear, cap."

"Of course Mole fell an easy victim to the unknown. He was drunk early in the day, and they made away with him without much trouble."

"Who's 'they'?"

"Well, he, she, it—I can't tell any more than you, but I say 'they,' because it looks like a planned thing, requiring more than one to carry it out," replied Jack.

"That's so," answered Hank.

They sat down to supper.

It was a melancholy meal, and they ate but little.

In spite of Mr. Mole's faults, they liked him, and there was a sense of chilling loneliness about the camp after losing three of its principal members.

What made it more awful and terror-inspiring, was the mystery surrounding the disappearances.

"By gosh! kernel," said Hank, breaking a silence which had become oppressive, "things are looking serious."

"I guess they are," replied Jack.

"Who's goin' to stay home to-morrow?"

"I'm de boy!" cried Monday. "No ghost scare this child."

"Wall," said Hank, "I'm admiring your courage, and we'll see what you can do."

"Why not all stay?" replied Jack.

"Jes' as yer say, cap."

"If we are attacked, the three of us will be better than one."

"That's so."

"I don't want any help," said Monday, drawing his sharp, gleaming knife, which flashed in the fire-flames. "Cut throat mighty quick. Got to let um alone, I tell yer."

"Very well," said Jack. "You shall stop to-morrow, Monday, and if you should be gone when we return, Hank and I will explore the mystery."

"You rescue me, Mast Jack?"

"If it is in the power of mortal man, but we can't do impossibilities."

"Can't fight the power of darkness, cap," said Hank.

"Oh! nonsense. There is nothing supernatural about it"

"Can't say for sure," Hank rejoined, with a shake of the head.

That night passed in perplexity and doubt, as the others had done, and at daybreak they were astir.

The unseen enemy did not disturb them.

They resembled the fable of the bundle of sticks—together they could not be broken, but singly they could be attacked and vanquished.

Monday was left in charge of the camp, and Jack with Hank started once more after the bear-meat.

They hurried home.

Neither of them spoke, though one thought was uppermost in the minds of each.

Would Monday be there to welcome them back?

Jack feared not, and he had not the heart to wind his horn.

"Hello! Monday!" he exclaimed.

There was no answer.

"By thunder!" said Hank, "they've taken the Malay, too."

Eagerly they reached the camp.

Monday was gone as completely, as thoroughly, as the other members of the party.

"Say, cap, what's this?" said Hank.

He pointed to the ground.

There were signs of a struggle.

More than that.

Some dark-looking fluid had soaked into the frozen earth.

"Blood!" said Jack.

"And warm, too," replied Hank. "If it had not been hot, it wouldn't have eaten into the frozen airth like this."

"You're right."

"The black's used his knife."

"Perhaps it's his own blood," said Jack.

"May be."

"It settles one question," continued Jack. "We have no ghosts to fight against, but a denizen of the world like ourselves. Spirits don't use knives, nor can weapons let blood out of them."

"Let you and I stop together next day," replied Hank.

"You bet we will."

They ate their supper, and kept watch and watch till morning, the biting winter blast soughing in melancholy cadence through the branches of the pine-trees, and the leaden sky frowning down upon them.

The following day they remained at home.

But nothing came near the camp.

They were sadly disappointed.

"This is the work of one person," said Jack, "and he or she dare not attack two together."

"That's jes' what I think," said Hank.

For a whole week they did not move away.

But their curiosity was not gratified.

The unseen enemy kept away from them.

At length, Jack could bear the tedium of staying in camp no longer.

"I wish a thaw would come and melt the snow," he exclaimed, "so that I could explore these hills. If they should be full of gold ore, what a rush there would be from the Gai!"

"Yes, and from all parts of the States," answered Hank.

"I shall take my rifle and go out for an hour"

"You might get some hares."

"I won't be away long, Hank. You won't be scared?"

"Not I, cap. You never saw me scared," replied the old hunter. "That's not my style of doing business."

Jack said no more, but, putting on his snow-shoes, he started, rifle in hand, for a brisk walk along the valley.

He had not gone far before he fancied that the wind bore towards him a mournful cry.

"What's the matter now?" inquired the Professor.

"Got to come out, sah."

"Let me alone. Who says so?"

"De govner's orders."

"I'm the only governor here," replied Mr. Mole. "So take your hands off.

"Come out here, sah."

"I'll not do it, Monday. Be still. Stop, won't you?"

Monday made no answer.

Exerting all his strength, he jerked Mr. Mole out of the waggon, and he fell sprawling on his back at Jack's feet.

"This is an outrage!" he cried.

"Aren't you ashamed of yourself, sir, to impose on good nature?" asked Jack. "Fall in at once between Hank and Monday. Now, boys, make a start. Indian file. Off you go!"

"Hold on, Jack," said Mr. Mole, "I've left my flask in the waggon."

"It will stay there."

"But——"

"Fall in!"

"Where are my snow-shoes?"

"Right before you. Put them on."

The Professor obeyed with a bad grace, and the party soon afterwards started, Hank leading the way, Mole going next, and Monday and Jack bringing up the rear.

Once or twice Jack turned round and looked back at the camp, to remark the melancholy figure of Harvey standing out all alone, as he leant on his rifle and cast his eyes on the ground.

They had the cold, bitter, biting wind right in their faces, and it chilled them to the marrow of their bones.

The dull, heavy, lowering sky was full of more snow, which would assuredly fall as soon as the wind went down.

No one spoke.

The weary journey was made in silence.

Hank followed the track of the previous day, and experienced no difficulty in reaching the cave.

The stone was rolled away, and the meat was found frozen stiff.

But what was very sorrowful was, that the cubs, deprived of warmth and nourishment, had died in the night.

They were frozen stiff.

Like the babes in the wood, they had sought consolation in one another's arms, and were lying side by side and face to face.

"Poor beasts!" said Hank. "That'd make a pictur' for an artist. Look at the little things. See how closely they cuddle up. Look at that one's paw round the other one's neck. I tell yer, fellows, there is a lot of affection 'bout animals, if yer did but know it!"

Delivering himself of this speech, Hank spoilt the picture by tossing a cub on to the snow, and following it up to skin it.

"You're rather rough on your picture!" exclaimed Jack.

"Wal, it's business, kernel. Cub eats good, and I reckon we shouldn't gain much by weepin' over the little things. It's what we've all got to come to."

A couple of yards off stood the Professor, who was in a bad temper, and only too glad of a chance of annoying the hunter.

"Do you mean we've all got to come to skinning?" he asked.

"No, dyin'," was the reply.

"Why don't you say what you mean?"

"You always were a skin!" said Hank, cutting away with his knife.

"Wear a skin!" repeated the Professor, affecting to misunderstand his words. "Of course I do. I couldn't go about in flesh and bones, could I?"

"Ah, pshaw! you know what I mean?"

"Indeed, I do not. Have the kindness to explain yourself, my imaginatical friend."

Hank turned round and faced Mr. Mole.

"Now," said he, "I want you to stop. Don't call me no sich names, because I won't have it. Ef yer want to swear at me, do it in English, but when it comes to calling a man a 'hen egg mattical,' yer might as well sit on me and hatch me out for what I'm worth."

"He didn't mean any harm," said Jack.

"Darn it, kernel, when he calls a man a mathematical hen egg, it's time to close."

"You'll make something of it presently," said Mr. Mole.

"You can't play upon me, Professor," answered Hank, "and I want yer to know it."

He brandished his bloody knife as he spoke, and the Professor retreated in dismay, tumbling back into a snow-bank, out of which he scrambled with much loss of dignity.

Hank went to work again, and when each member of the party was supplied with a load, they started for home.

The sun was just setting, and it had shone out for a brief space like a cold and lifeless orb in the far off west, as they reached the camp.

"Hello, Dick!" cried Jack.

There was no answer.

"Toot yer horn, squire," said Hank. "Mebbe he's fretting inside of a tent."

Jack had his horn with him, and he blew a loud blast on it.

"To-hoot—to-hoo—to-hoo—o—o!"

Still there was no response.

The silence was as oppressive as that of the grave.

With sad forebodings they entered the small space they had marked off as a camp.

Jack looked eagerly in every tent.

There was no sign of Harvey.

"Good God!" he exclaimed. "What does this mean?"

"I'll allow it's kinder cur'us," said Hank.

As before, on the disappearance of Hilda, they examined the surrounding snow, and looked in the waggon.

The snow had not been disturbed, no stores were gone, and the mules were quietly eating the hay which had been thrown them in the corral.

There were no traces of a struggle.

Harvey had disappeared as mysteriously as had Hilda.

"Gone to join his wife in the happy hunting-grounds," said Mr. Mole.

"Don't you chaff," replied Jack. "It may be your turn next."

"Nonsense," answered the Professor. "You can't frighten me with your ghosts and hobgoblins. I'm dead beat. I want to rest, and I'll keep camp to-morrow. Give me powder and bullets, and I'll knock spots out of everything from this world or the world of spirits, if it interferes with me. All I want is the key of the whisky barrel."

"And all I want," said Jack, "is the key to this enigma."

"Think it out, Jack," replied Mr. Mole. "Think it out. You were always good at riddles when you were only a little boy."

"I'll take you at your word, sir," replied Jack. "How?"

swing him backward and forward three times, and then, when I say 'three,' let him go. Do you see?"

"All right," replied Gosh.

The boat was going at a good pace, considering that there was little or no wind, and everything seemed to favour their purpose; but just as they were preparing to throw Harkaway in the sea, Gosh, who was looking over the starboard side of the boat, exclaimed—

"Hold hard, mate!"

"What's the matter now?" asked Spanish Joe.

"Why, just this. We were as near putting our foot in it as possible. It's lucky I happened to catch sight of the craft or there would have been a witness of the—the murder!—ugh! how I hate that word!—and most likely we should have had our necks stretched for our trouble."

Spanish Joe looked round in obedience to his companion's hint, and saw a boat considerably bigger than their own.

It was somewhat extraordinary that they should not have noticed it before, for it was within three hundred yards of them.

Its sole occupant was a man of commanding mien and tall stature.

He wore a thick pilot jacket, with brass buttons. His hat was a flat-crowned oilskin.

He was standing up, with the tiller in one hand and a double-barrelled fowling-piece in the other.

It was evident that the movements of those in the other boat interested him deeply.

"Drop the bloat and stop his mouth! We shall have the fellow down on us else!" exclaimed Spanish Joe, in hurried accents.

Jack was instantly released, and allowed to fall heavily upon the timbers of the boat.

Although the fall hurt him, he did not leave off shouting for assistance at the top of his voice.

He, too, had seen the strange boat, and wild hopes of rescue sprang up in his breast.

"Hold your row, will you?" exclaimed Gosh.

"No, no! Help, help!" cried Jack. "Save me, sa——!"

He was unable to complete the sentence, for Gosh gave him a brutal kick in the side, which deprived him of breath and nearly broke his ribs.

"That will teach you to hold your tongue. You had better shut up, I can tell you, my lad, or I'll give you another dose, which might have the effect of stopping your jaw for ever. I should be sorry to hurt a promising chap like yourself; but just at this moment we want as little noise as possible."

The stranger continued to steer his boat in the direction of the ruffians.

Jack was silent.

He was too much hurt to be able to speak or cry out.

Every now and then he gasped painfully, as if he was injured internally.

"I say, what's that?" said Spanish Joe, pointing to a locker in the stern. "Won't that hold him? Just step up to it and see what size it is."

Gosh opened the door and disclosed a capacious sort of cupboard, in which was a coil of rope, a jar containing some tar, a small bag of nails, and a hammer.

"It'll do fine" said Gosh.

"Bundle him in, then, neck and crop, and look slippery, for blessed if I don't think that fellow 'uded in Queer-street, if we don't look out. Have you silenced the boat, do you think?"

"He is quiet enough," replied Gosh. "I gave him a rib-roaster with one of my hob-nailed boots, and I think he is disposed of for the next quarter of an hour."

"Shove him in, then, neck and crop."

Gosh required no further bidding.

He took Jack up by the shoulders, and giving him a cast forward, threw him into the locker, immediately afterwards shutting the door and fastening it securely by turning the button which held it on the outside.

This was no sooner brought to a satisfactory conclusion than the stranger exclaimed, in a loud voice, putting his hands to his mouth, speaking trumpet-fashion—

"Ahoy, there! Boat ahoy!"

"All right, guv'nor," replied Spanish Joe. "You have no cause to hurt your lungs. We're a-listening."

"Stand-to!" shouted the stranger.

"Oh, no! Why should we? The lake's as much ours as yours, and we have as much right to it as you have. We are in our own boat, and haven't done you any harm, so we shan't stand-to for anybody."

"If you don't," the stranger said, in a clear commanding voice, "I shall feel it my duty to make you."

"You're a nice sort of pirate, I don't think," responded Spanish Joe. "Why, you're as bad as Paul Jones or Captain Kydd."

He dropped his voice, and added to his companion—

"If it wasn't for his gun and if I were alongside of him with a few inches of cold steel, he'd have bad luck."

A sinister expression stole over his face, and there was little doubt that he meant what he said.

But the fellow was, like most bravos, at heart a coward, and the sight of a gun, which he surmised was loaded, rather alarmed him, and made him more cautious than he otherwise would have been, though it did not check the insolence of his tongue.

"Furl your sail," said the stranger.

"It's all very well to say furl it, but I'm blessed if I know how to," grumbled Joe.

"Here, let me do it," said Gosh. "I think we ought to let go that rope. I'll try it, at all events."

He undid the rope he spoke of, and the sail was soon lying in a heap, partly in the boat, and partly out of it, as a portion of the canvas, not being well directed in its descent, dragged in the water.

In a few seconds the stranger was alongside, and holding on by the end of a boat-hook.

He did not attempt to board the boat.

His gun rested by his side.

With one hand he steered, and with the other he held on to the vessel, which he may be said to have captured.

The two ruffians could not help being impressed by the fine handsome face of the man to whom they had been forced to succumb. He was a type of a different class than that to which they belonged. There was little that was bad in that face. It was a good, generous, and noble face.

"Now, my men, listen to me," exclaimed the stranger, as the two boats flew along together

that the pain of Hunston's wound allowed him to utter.

"Have you anything else to tell me?" he asked.

Hunston related how Pe-bo-a had captured her prisoners, and also her remarks about Harkaway finding the Secret of Wealth, which was hidden away in a stone coffin in some corner of the vast ramifications of caverns known as the Kehamas.

"Your life is your own," replied Jack. "I believe all you have told me, and am grateful to you for the information, which is of the utmost value to me."

"I told you I wouldn't lie," replied Hunston.

"If you had I would have blown your brains out."

"Is there anything else I can enlighten you on?"

"No."

"Then, for God's sake, give me something to stop this hemorrhage, or I shall bleed to death. Look at the snow—it is all melted with hot blood. I must have some important artery severed by your infernally unlucky shot."

Jack went into a tent and returned with a shirt, which he tore into strips, and bound tightly round the injured limb.

Hunston winced under the operation, but it gave him relief, and stopped the faintness which was stealing over him.

It was time for Jack now to turn his attention to Pe-bo-a.

He did so.

She had crawled to the edge of the crater.

What she intended to do he knew not, though he imagined she wished to get back into the cave and put her prisoners to death before he could rescue them.

She heard him approach.

The sound of his footsteps on the hard, frozen ground seemed to stimulate her to increased exertions.

She was already hanging by one hand, the other being severed, to the top of the pit.

"Stop, stop!" he cried.

Possibly his voice frightened her, and she may have suspected he wanted to kill her.

However that may be, her hold slipped, and she fell into the gulf below.

Down, down, away down!

Jack peered after, awe-stricken, and her despairing cries and groans, as her body bounded from side to side, rang in his ears for many a night afterwards, as he lay in his tent listening to the mournful howl of the coyote, and the sharp shriek of the bitter wintry blasts.

There was no doubt that she was dead.

He turned away with a sickening sensation.

"Where's the old girl?" asked Hunston sitting up.

"Gone down the crater."

"The deuce she has! How did that happen?"

"Lost her grip when she heard me coming," answered Jack.

"Let her go; she's no loss. Can't I go into one of your tents and be covered up?"

"Why, certainly."

"I'm nearly frozen here, and feel as weak as a rat, though I'm not in so much pain since you bandaged me up."

"I'll put you in Monday's tent, and cover you with skins; that'll warm you."

"Good enough. If you should ever be in the same fix, I'll think of you."

"Oh! I'm a white man," replied Jack, "and don't wan't to be hard on a fallen enemy. When you're well again, I'll give you fits."

"Or I will you," said Hunston.

"Ah, pshaw! You're as bad as, or worse than, your brother. Let's be friends. I've no quarrel with you."

"Be friends with you?"

"Yes. Shake hands."

"No, sir," replied Hunston, while a look of unutterable aversion crossed his face. "I'll never be friendly with you."

"As you please," said Jack, with a careless shrug of the shoulders. "It don't make the difference of a row of pins to me."

"Anyhow, I'll take advantage of this truce," answered Hunston, "and make all the use I can of you. Have you got a drop of whisky in your store-waggon?"

"Yes."

"Hand it out, then. I'm so faint with loss of blood that I can scarcely crawl."

"Wait a while," replied Jack.

He took him up in his arms, and carried him, as if he had been a little child, to Monday's tent, where he wrapped him in skins, and made him as comfortable as he could, afterwards giving him some whisky and a paper of chewing tobacco.

For the latter Hunston was very thankful.

"Thank you, old boy," he said. "I wish I could like you, and wipe out my grudge, but I can't."

"Are you all right?" asked Jack.

"Hunky dorey, thanks."

"How do I go down to the Kehamas, as you call them?" continued Jack.

"Easy enough. You will see holes and supports in the right-hand wall of the crater, conducting to a ledge of rock. This ledge leads to the cavern.

"Where are the prisoners?"

"In a chamber on the north side of the first cave. A rock is rolled against the door. Push it back."

"Good," said Jack.

He left Hunston and proceeded to follow his instructions, which speedily landed him in the cavern.

A glance round showed him the rock.

Rolling it aside, his knife was rapidly busy with the withes forming the bonds of the captives and the whole of them left the vault, assembling in the adjoining cavern.

Jack embraced his wife tenderly.

Young Jack was wild with joy, and the others crowded around Harkaway, shaking him by the hand, and overwhelming him with questions.

Briefly he responded, telling them all that had happened.

"I always said pop was the biggest man on this continent!" exclaimed Young Jack, "and now I know it."

CHAPTER XXI.

THE SECRET OF WEALTH.

"HE has cast all his former achievements into the shade by this one," remarked Mr. Mole.

"Um done um real smart thing!" exclaimed Monday.

"Dat am de truest word ever you spoke," replied Pete.

Harvey and Hilda were too happy to speak.

Viola clung lovingly to Jack, and all she could say, was:—

"Oh, my dear, dear husband, we meet again."

Mr. Mole exclaimed:—

"I move the adjournment of this debate. We're all dying of thirst and hunger."

edge, they soon stood on the very brink.

Jack looked down below.

All was black as night.

He raised a ponderous stone and let it drop.

It went down, down, down!

There was no sound of splashing, as there would have been had it gone down a well.

Nor did it strike anything but the jagged and unequal sides.

A heavy, rumbling, thunderous noise arose, and that was all.

"I give it as my belief," said Mole, "that this shaft goes deep down into the bowels of the earth. Who knows what its hidden recesses might reveal?"

"Perhaps the Secret of Wealth," replied Jack.

"Possibly."

Hank's voice recalled them to the camp.

"Say cap!" he exclaimed, "ef yer goin' ter waste the hull day with that old fossil talkin' about volcaners, why we'll fire inter our hash without yer."

Mr. Mole bent an indignant glance upon Hank.

"Call me an old fossil, will you?" he said.

"That's just what I said, Professor, and I'm not runnin'! I'm standing right here."

"I'd have you to know that I'm a man o science."

"That's what yer say; but what does all yer science amount ter, anyway?"

"A great deal."

"Can yer tell what weather we re goin' ter hev?"

"No. I am not a meteorologist."

"Meat-yer. I can't get my mouth in shape for that. It's a big word, and I guess it means a heap," replied Hank, with a shake of the head. "But talkin' of meat, yer mind me on this we're goin' to hev snow."

"Ha! ha! ha!" laughed Mole.

"What air yer grinnin' at, professor, for all the world like the orang-outrang at a show, when yer hand him a bit of candy or an apple?"

"What has snow to do with our meat supply?"

"Everything."

"Prove it."

"I will," said Hank. "Look here, we're run out of fresh meat, ain't we."

"Yes."

"And we ain't been able to kill nothin' at all since we've pitched our camp on these hyar parts."

"That's so."

"But yer don't suppose as this island is destitute of fresh meat. Yer won't go to say that there ain't no bars, no deer, and sich, with perhaps a panther er two?"

"I shouldn't think you would find anything of the sort."

"That just shows yer ignorance."

"How?"

"Aren't there all them animals in the Black Hills?"

"Yes, but we're on an island, and is it likely they would swim over?" asked Mole.

"Swim, is it?" replied Hank.

"Yes; answer me that."

"No, they wouldn't."

"That's where I've got you, as sure as Saint Patrick, of blessed memory, cleared all the snakes out of Ireland," said Mole, rubbing his hands and

a cheap victory over his old enemy, Hank.

"Now, look a-hear!" exclaimed Hank. "Couldn't they cross over on the ice when the lake's froze hard in Winter?"

Mr. Mole did not make any reply.

"He had you there, sir," said Harvey.

"Yes," said Jack, "that's one for Hank."

"Let the man go on. Talk's cheap," replied the Professor.

"If it's cheap, mine's good," continued Hank; "and I tell you that if we hev a fall of snow, as I expect, in four-and-twenty hours, p'rap' l ss, we shall hev the tracks of bars to follow up, ad this camp will hev fresh pervisions."

This argument was unanswerable, and the Professor, grumbling to himself, walked back to the square piece of rock which served as a table, and prepared himself for the midday meal.

Hank was right.

Toward the evening, the lowering clouds, driven by a heavy wind, swept close to the earth.

Then the wind dropped.

A leaden, murky sky, growing denser and thicker, hung overhead, and the clouds closed in all round, indicating the approach of a storm.

Monday had cut down a pine-tree and chopped it up into logs.

The fire was piled up high, and blazed brightly.

The mules which had drawn the wagon were safely corraled hard by, and five clear white tents, forming a semicircle, with the waggon in the centre and the fire ahead of that, made the camp.

At eight o'clock all turned in.

One tent was Jack's, the second Harvey and Hilda's, the third Monday's, and the fourth Hank's, while the Professor had the fifth to himself.

They were all comfortable enough, with plenty of blankets, and were in a much better position than they had been during many portions of their lives during their wanderings and adventures.

Jack was very cold and hard in his manner.

He grieved for the loss of his wife and son.

Little did he dream that they were even at that moment on the other side of the island in the lake, held in thrall by Hunston and Olalla.

Nor did he imagine for a moment that Fannie, the Blonde Beauty, the intriguing wife of the dead Cabuchon, had married Hunston, and was sai g round the island to go and torment Viola and domineer over Young Jack.

It was as well for him that he did not know these things.

Had he done so, the fever of his brain would have been increased, and it would have made him still more miserable.

As it was, he was sad enough.

Although he had been some time on the island in the lake, he had not yet come near solving its mystery.

Where was the Secret of Wealth?

He remembered the words of the old Indian woman, M rama, at A e-we-an-pe, who predicted with her dying breath that he was the one man destined to solve this mystery.

Perhaps he was on the threshold of great discoveries.

Who could tell?

It was impossible to say what a day might bring forth.

During the night snow fell heavily in thick, blinding flakes.

The storm continued all the next day, and Monday was constantly employed in removing the snow, which, when the storm was over, lay believe that they have one quality to save them from eternal perdition; and yet those who know them intimately, and have studied their characters closely and critically, know that they are occasionally devoted in their friendship, and generous to a fault.

The man who would commit a murder without compunction, and shed blood like water, without a sigh or a shudder, would share his last crust with a friend, and fight like a madman in his defence.

The ruffian hobbled along, and continued to groan at intervals.

The distance was short, and he was glad when he succeeded in traversing it.

"Hello, mate!" exclaimed Shadrach, when he saw his guests approaching. "You've got a lame leg. Is it broke?"

"No, it isn't so bad as that; but some fellow who was out shooting put a charge of shot into it. Bless him! I should like to come across him, that's all. Perhaps I shall, some day. Anyhow, I'll live in hopes, and if we do meet, it'll be the worse for him, that's all I've got to say; for I'll take my oath both of us don't survive that meeting!"

There was a savage energy about the man as he delivered himself of this speech.

"I suppose you were doing something to the chap," said Shadrach, with a half-smile.

Spanish Joe seemed willing that the charcoal-burners should believe the hypothesis they had suggested, for he made no answer.

The night was becoming very cold.

The wind had suddenly veered round to the north-east, and a biting, keen and wintry blast swept through the branches of the trees, making the men shiver as they sat round the fire.

Bendigo good-naturedly placed a bundle of leaves and dry grass at Joe's service, saying—

"You'll be easier on that than on the bare earth, and I'm sure you're welcome to it, if so be as you'll have it."

Joe looked up at him thankfully, and replied:

"I'm your debtor, and will do as much for you some day, if I have the chance."

"What will you have for supper? We've a bit of mutton, if you like to cut off some slices, and broil it over the fire," said Shadrach.

Gosh accepted this offer of something to eat, for he was hungry.

What remained of the stolen sheep was brought out of the hut, and Gosh helped himself, cutting off as much as he thought his friend and himself would be able to consume.

He threw the slices of juicy meat upon the glowing embers, and one of the charcoal-burners lent him a sharp-pointed stick with which to turn the meat over when he thought one side was done enough.

Plates and knives and forks there were none.

The charcoal-burners ate their meat with their fingers, tearing it with their teeth after the manner of wild beasts; but Joe had a knife in his pocket, and with that the ruffians carved their victuals in a less cannibal-like manner.

When the rough meal was over, the charcoal-burners produced a demijohn containing whisky, which they offered to their new acquaintance.

Spanish Joe did not drink much, for he was afraid of inflaming his wound.

But Gosh indulged freely, and became boisterously merry.

The others fell into a drunken slumber around the fire, much later in the night, and awoke the next morning with aching heads and burning throats.

On examination, Spanish Joe's wounds were found to be much inflamed, and he expressed his determination to stay a day or two where he was, if the charcoal-burners would let him.

They made no objection, and Shadrach obtained some water from a spring which welled up hard by, and placing it by the wounded man's side in a pannikin. Joe took off his neckerchief and bathed his wounds whenever they felt hot and feverish.

Towards the evening, suppuration commenced, and he did not suffer so much as he had done hitherto.

Gosh grew impatient of living in the woods, and panted for action and the delights of the Crow's Nest once more.

But they were delights which were not forthcoming.

He could not desert his friend, and there seemed every probability of his being compelled to stay in the woods for some days, perhaps weeks, to come.

But he was not destined to be long without excitement.

Harkaway had made inquiries for Spanish Joe down at the Gap, and all the information he could obtain was that neither Joe nor his friend Gosh had been seen lately in their usual haunts.

Naturally, Jack imagined that they were afraid to show up.

He concluded they were hiding in the woods.

Without saying a word to anyone regarding his determination, he resolved to go after the villain.

This was thoroughly characteristic of Jack.

He did not want any help.

Two to one made no difference to him.

He would not have hesitated to fight a giant, if he had come across one.

Besides this, he was desperate.

He had very little to live for, since his wife and child were gone, and all that consoled him and reconciled him to life was the excitement which his wild way of living brought with it.

So he shouldered his rifle and started for the woods, to see if he could not hunt out Spanish Joe and his cowardly confederate.

He had not gone far in the woods before he happened to strike the charcoal-burners' camp.

Shadrach and Bendigo were absent.

They had gone to the Gap with charcoal.

Spanish Joe was inside the hut, asleep, and Gosh was sitting at the fireside, sometimes stirring the logs and sometimes whittling a stick.

Jack had an eye like a hawk.

No sooner did he see Gosh than he recognised him as the man who had forced him on board the boat.

"Ha! I've found you sooner than I expected," exclaimed Jack.

Gosh turned round.

His countenance fell.

"It's the bloat," he muttered.

In a moment, he drew his pistol and fired at Jack, missing him by an inch.

The latter in self-defence, raised his rifle to a level with his hip, and gave Gosh a rough and ready shot.

She had made holes in the rocks for hands to grasp and feet to rest on, and, with these helps, she drew herself up

"Follow me," she said.

When her head was on a level with the surface, she looked down, and continued—

"He is in his tent. He sleeps, perhaps."

"Go on," said Olalla.

The next moment Pe-bo-a was on the solid ground, and Olalla and Hunston, who followed him closely, were by her side.

There were no signs of Harkaway.

The white tents were visible close by, but the camp appeared deserted.

Perhaps the old woman was right in her surmise, and Jack, worn out by fatigue, had gone to sleep.

If so, he would fall an easy prey to his enemies.

The three then advanced.

Suddenly the ping of a bullet was heard.

Olalla sprang into the air, uttered the war-cry of his nation, and fell down dead.

So perished the last of the Bannocks.

Hunston fired in the direction of the smoke, though he could see nobody.

Another shot came from the same direction.

A ball struck Hunston in the leg, and he fell to the ground, writhing in agony.

His leg was broken.

Pe-bo-a tried to regain the mouth of the crater.

But, with a loud laugh, Harkaway stepped from behind a tent, rifle in hand, and, running behind her, cut off her retreat.

He had a tomahawk in his hand.

She had a knife.

With considerable dexterity she tried to cut him with it.

He avoided her thrusts, and, with one blow of his tomahawk, severed her hand from her arm, cutting the wrist in two.

The hand, still tightly clutching the knife, dropped to the ground, while Pe-bo-a, who was bleeding freely, showered choice imprecations in her own language on Jack.

She sank on her side and writhed in agony.

Jack was about to wrap his kerchief round her wound, and bent down for that purpose, as he did not like to see an aged woman suffer.

This humane action, under Providence, saved his life.

Hunston had drawn his pistol and took aim at Jack

He fired just as he stooped.

The ball whistled harmlessly over his head.

With a huge bound, Jack stood before him.

Up to this time he had not known who it was he had shot, but his glance no sooner fell upon Hunston's well-known features then he uttered an exclamation of joy—

"At last," he exclaimed, "you are in my power. Put down that pistol, or I'll brain you."

He clubbed his rifle as he spoke.

Hunston had not time to fire another shot, and with a muttered curse he threw his pistol on the ground.

"Hit a man when he's down!" he said. "That's very manly, isn't it?"

"You'd shoot a man in the back, you reptile."

"I'd shoot you, any way and any how," said Hunston, boldly.

Jack smiled grimly.

did you?"

"No. He had faults enough, but he was not a coward, as you say," answered Jack. "I'm bound to admit that."

"My leg's broken, and yet I don't wince."

"Have you any more arms?"

"No."

Jack searched him and found this statement to be correct.

He removed the rifle and pistol, discharged them, and put them away.

"I guess you're harmless now," he said, "and you can't run far."

"Couldn't move to save my life," replied Hunston.

"Bone broken, eh?"

"No. I'm bleeding 'fore and aft, so I reckon the ball went through the fleshy part; but it don't matter much, as I suppose you'll kill me. Why don't you do it out of hand?"

"I'll spare your life on one condition."

"Name it."

"Answer all my questions faithfully."

"If I do, will you let me live?"

"Yes"

"And you won't make me swear to give up hunting you? If I did I shouldn't keep the oath."

"Oh, I don't care for you," replied Jack, affecting a disdain he did not really feel, for he knew Hunston to be really a formidable enemy, as he had proved himself all that on many occasions.

"Perhaps you'll talk differently some day."

"May be."

"Well, go on. What do you want to know?"

"Who's the old woman?"

"Pe-bo-a. Great Medicine. Lives in the Kehamas."

"What are they?"

"A chain of caves under the hill."

"Did you come from there, and how?"

"Yes, we came up that hole. Got steps. First cavern not more than a few feet from the surface."

"Who's that Indian I shot?"

"Olallo, the Corpse-maker."

"Is that so?" exclaimed Jack, much gratified at having killed the dreaded Corpse-Maker. "What brought you here?"

"I met Mrs. Cabuchon at Flyaway Gap and married her, taking her to our camp on the other side of the island."

"Married Fannie?"

"I did. We had as prisoners your wife and your child. Fannie had them beaten. Young Jack got mad and went for me. I tried to shoot him. We struggled, pistol went off, and Fannie was accidentally shot. Your wife, with Pete and Young Jack, escaped. We followed them to the Kehamas, where they had been made prisoners by Pe-bo-a."

"Has she any other prisoners?"

"Yes, all your friends."

"Are they alive?"

"They are."

"When did you reach the Kehamas, and when did you see the prisoners?"

"I did both about an hour ago," answered Hunston.

Jack was deeply excited.

Here was a budget of news for him, condensed into a few disjointed sentences, which were all

"Why, certainly."

"I had a dream last night," she continued.

"I had two, but hang me if I remember them," he replied, with a coarse laugh.

"Mine was about my husband."

"Jack Harkaway ?"

"Yes."

"What did you dream ?"

"I thought he was on this island, and I want you to promise me one thing."

"Well ?"

"If it should be a true dream, and you should meet with him, you will not kill him, if you have the chance ?"

"I don't know about that."

"Oh, promise me !"

She seized his arm, and looked up tearfully and supplicatingly in his face.

"Oh ! all right. I won't kill him," he said.

"Thank you. God bless you for that," she exclaimed.

He thought her dream was all nonsense.

It was not very likely that Jack would leave Ate-we-an-pe and get on the island.

At all events, his promise was only binding on him.

He might employ someone else to kill him.

"You will keep your word ?" she added.

"Yes."

"As God's your judge."

"Oh, yes. Mrs. Harkaway, make your mind easy on that point. I may have been a bad young man. I believe I am, in some respects. But if I say a thing, I mean it."

Viola breathed a sigh of relief.

Hunston started on his long walk.

He had, on a clear day, seen the range of hills which bisected the island, and came to the conclusion that it was useless to attempt to cross them as they were covered with snow.

So he determined to walk round by the beach, and see if he could not make the circuit of the island.

For five days he walked steadily, building up his camp-fire at night, cooking any game he had killed, or supping on the provisions he carried in his bag.

At dusk he wrapped himself up in his blanket, and slept, like an Indian, on the ground.

Thanks to a young and healthy constitution, this did not hurt him.

Though he had lost one eye, he did not seem to feel the loss much.

The sight in the other was quickened.

It was the disfigurement he hated.

His vanity was hurt, just as Lord Mossbunker was hurt at the loss of his two ears.

He often said to himself—

"I'll get square with Harkaway for this. It was his fault. If I had not been captured by him, and taken into Ate-we-an-pe, it would not have happened. He made my brother a one-armed man, and I am a one-eyed one. A wall-eyed beast. Curse Harkaway. I'll get up sticks with him if I die for it."

On the morning of the sixth day, he had travelled so far by the shore that he came to Flyaway Gap.

By a singular coincidence, the first man he saw was Spanish Joe.

And yet it was not so singular, after all.

Spanish Joe was a loafer.

Hunston met him a little way out of the settlement, for he could see the wooden shanties before him

"Say, stranger !" exclaimed Joe. "What's your little game ?"

"I don't know— do you ?" replied Hunston.

"You wall-eyed cuss," answered Joe, "can't you give a civil answer to a civil question ?"

"I'll give you the lead," said Hunston, " if you guy me on that blind eye of mine."

In a moment Spanish Joe drew a revolver, and pointed it at Hunston.

"Say that again, and you're a dead man—so help me Christopher Columbus," he said.

Hunston was alarmed.

"I—I—did not mean anything," he stammered.

"All right, my hearty. 'Nother time, don't say what you don't mean," said Joe.

But he kept his pistol in his hand, and his eye on Hunston.

"Seems to me," continued Hunston, " as if you don't often see strangers in these parts."

"Oh, yes, we do."

"When did the last come ?"

"But a month ago ; quite a batch of them."

"Who were they ?"

"Jack Harkaway and friends, with a lot of Indians as hangers-on."

Hunston gave a start.

"Hey !" exclaimed Spanish Joe. "What's up ? Trod on a sand-adder ?"

"No," replied Hunston, recovering his presence of mind. "I've got a bad corn. It hurts me now and again. I think it's going to rain. It always touc es me up in wet weather."

"Maybe" said Joe. "If it ain't an impertinence, where did you come from ?"

"Other side of the Island."

"How ?"

"I'm a hunter, and struck this place by chance."

"Never seen our settlement ?"

"No."

"Oh, it's fine. Bang-up, I tell you. Flyaway Gap is all a place. Come with me, and I'll trate you dacent, as the song says."

"Not now," said Hunston. "Where can I find you, if I want you ?"

"What for ?"

"That's my business."

"Got any stamps "

"A few."

"Well, you can go to the Gap, and ask for Spanish Joe at a saloon called the " Little Brown Jug," or you can come on to the Crow's Nest, which is a wooden shanty where half a score of the toughs live. We're the hardest crowd in the Gap, I tell you, and don't you forget it."

"Not particular ?"

"Not a darned bit, so long as we scoop in the ducats."

"Then you're the man for me."

"I don't know exactly what you mean, squire," said Spanish Joe, " but I can only repeat I'm all there when I'm wanted."

"Good enough. What is this place you call the Gap ?"

"Mining settlement."

" Been here long ?"

"Close on a year."

"Get any gold ?"

"Lots, if you choose to work for it."

"Many of you ?"

"Half a thousand—men, women, and children."

spilled one drop of J........

He wanted to take him ... with him safe and sound, so that he might reserve him for the torture and the death that he intended to put him to.

"Get up," he said to Jack. "We'll be getting on board this boat, or the owner may come up and change my plans."

He thought he could skirt the island in the boat.

This would save him the labour of going round on foot, in the way he had come.

It was a good idea.

Jack rose.

His arms were bound behind him, and he could make no resistance

Suddenly there was a loud cry.

Spanish Joe fell to the ground, with a tomahawk deeply imbedded in his brain.

He never moved again.

The villain was sent before his supreme Judge with all his sins upon his head.

No time was given him for repentance.

An Indian, who had been concealed behind the Giant's Rock, had sprung upon him as he passed.

One blow of the upraised tomahawk had caused his awfully sudden death.

Both Jack and Hunston turned round at the cry.

The latter paled, but grasped his rifle firmly.

Jack smiled.

In the Indian he recognised Ghost-that-lies-in-the-Wood.

His luck had not deserted him yet.

Still was his good star in the ascendant.

When Ghost saw Hunston's movement, he also raised his rifle.

"Stop that!" exclaimed the Indian.

Hunston scowled, but did not attempt to fire, for the simple reason that, as Ghost spoke, six other Indians appeared upon the scene.

They were all armed.

He would have little chance against so many, if he began hostilities.

Ghost-that-lies-in-the-Wood did not travel unattended.

The Indian was greatly excited.

He walked up to Hunston and seized him angrily by the arm.

"Why did you do this?" he asked.

"Because he is my enemy," replied Hunston. "Take your dirty paws off me. Do you hear?"

Ghost shook him.

Hunston was also very angry and desperate.

He struck Ghost a violent blow in the face with his fist, and a scuffle ensued between them.

At such close quarters they were unable to use their weapons.

Ghost-that-lies-in-the-Wood seemed like a feather in Hunston's hands.

He was not strong.

Hunston was surprised at this, and got him by the throat.

With a desperate effort Ghost broke away, but Hunston dragged his blanket from him, and tore off an undershirt he wore, stripping him naked to the waist.

"Hello!" cried Hunston. "What's this?"

Ghost covered his breast with his hands, and sank on his knees.

No wonder Hunston was surprised.

Ghost-that-lies-in-the-Wood was not a man!

Hunston had disclosed the *form of a woman!*

This redoubtable chief belonged to the weaker sex.

What a disclosure!

The upper part of the body had been dyed red, but the breast and arms were white.

Here was another revelation.

Pushing Hunston rudely on one side, Jack exclaimed—

"Who and what are you?"

The pretended Indian made no reply.

Jack picked up the blanket, out of a feeling of delicacy, and handed it to Ghost-that-lies-in-the-Wood.

The eyes sought him as if to thank him, and then fell quickly, as if from shame.

Hunston saw a chance of escape.

Spanish Joe was dead, and could be of no further use to him.

If he would escape, he must do so quickly, and take advantage of Jack's preoccupation.

So he glided stealthily away, and jumping into the boat which was lying along shore, shoved her off, twisted the sail, and was soon out of gun-fire on the lake.

What the mystery was about Ghost-that-lies-in-the-Wood he could not even faintly guess.

He would have given worlds to stay and gratify his curiosity, but he did not dare to, as he felt convinced that Jack would attend to him as soon as he had an opportunity.

Harkaway did not bestow a thought upon Hunston.

He was watching the exposed Indian with an earnest gaze, and as soon as the blanket was drawn over the delicate shoulders he spoke.

"I know your secret," he said.

"Yes," replied Ghost-that-lies-in-the-Wood. "I am an Indian maiden, and not one of the Sioux among whom I have lived ever imagined me anything but a man."

"I do not mean that."

"What then?"

"You are no Indian."

"Who am I, then?"

"You are Mrs. Cabuchon, the wife of the guide. You are the Blonde Beauty. You——"

"Mr. Harkaway!"

"Hush!" he continued, interrupting her. "Denials are useless. All that was formerly mysterious is now clear. I often wondered how you could meet Mrs. Cabuchon and bring us together, but now I see that Fannie and Ghost-that-Lies-in-the-Wood are one and the same person, all wonder and bewilderment are at an end."

Again she cast down her eyes.

"Confess!" he cried.

"I do," she replied.

"You are Mrs. Cabuchon?"

"I am that unhappy woman."

"Your reasons for coming out here to the Black Hills?"

"They were twofold."

"How?"

"Firstly, I—I love you. I wanted to be near you and watch over you," she replied.

"Secondly?" said Jack.

"I had sworn to have revenge on my husband."

"And you killed him in the teepee at Olalla's camp?"

"I did

Olalla.

"Who are they?" demanded the chief.

"Can you not see?"

"I was too far behind you. Speak!"

"These are Young Jack, Pete, and Mrs. Harkaway——"

"How, how!"

"Harvey, Professor Mole, Hilda, Monday, and Hank Smith."

"Jack Harkaway's friends!"

"All of them."

"Where is Harkaway himself?" said Olalla.

"He is not there. I looked closely. Question the old hag. I want to know how they got into her power."

"O, Pe-bo-a!" said Olalla, "tell me in what manner you captured your prisoners."

"The first three have only been here a few hours," she replied.

"The woman, the boy, and the black man?"

"Yes. I found them asleep in the Kehamas, and I bound them one by one, pricking them with a knife to make them walk here."

"The others?"

"They were in camp near the shaft. I saw them one day when I was going out to seek food I waited till they were all out but one. That one became drowsy. I hit her with a stone, and lowered her with a rope on to the ledge of rock which projects into the shaft from this cavern. Each day one was left to guard the camp, I stole behind them, and felled them to the ground as I had done the first one."

"Is there not one left?"

"Yes."

"Why have you not got him?"

"He never sleeps. Every time I look over the edge of the shaft I find him, rifle in hand. He is a great chief."

"That is Harkaway," said Olalla.

A dark frown crossed the witch's face.

"Hark-a-wa!" she repeated. "That name has been whispered to me by the spirits of the dead. It has haunted me."

"What do the dead say?" inquired Olalla, much interested.

Like all his race, he was superstitious, and believed that the great medicine of the old woman enabled her to pry into future events.

"They tell me that Hark-a-wa will be the cause of my death."

"How, how?"

"When Hark-a-wa shall come I must go. I would not have touched these people if I had known they were with him. He will conquer me, and discover the Secret of Wealth."

"What is that?"

"In the Kehamas is the Secret of Wealth."

"Gold?"

The old woman shook her head.

"Silver?"

"No," she replied. "It is not red dirt or white dirt. I must not reveal its nature even to you O, Olalla."

"Where is it to be found? At least tell me that?"

"In one of the caves of the Kehamas is a vault, where great chiefs of the Indian tribes are buried. Years ago, when the Indian roamed free over this country, he occupied the Kesapa. No soldiers of the Tonkasila interfered with him But the Great Spirit grew angry with the red man, and by thunder and lightning drove him away from the Black Hills, and he has never entered it since."

"Yet you say traces of our occupation exist."

coffins, where the great dead are placed. Their bones rest in these stone graves, and in one of them will be found the Secret of Wealth."

Olalla smiled scornfully.

"What is this talk?" he said, with a laugh.

Pe-bo-a grew angry.

"Dare not to doubt the words of Pe-bo-a," she exclaimed, fiercely, while her eyes flashed like those of a snake. "I have said it, and the spirits have told me for years that Hark-a-wa should come from the East and obtain the secret of the red man."

"Have you seen it?"

"No mortal eye has seen it."

"How do you know all about it, then, O Pe-bo-a?"

"The tradition of the tribes has been handed down to me, and you, Olalla, ought to have heard it."

"I have," he replied, thoughtfully. "But I thought it so much nonsense."

"Did not great medicine go out of the Sioux lately?" she continued.

"How, how?"

"When Mir-a-ma died her spirit came to me, and she told me I should soon see Hark-a-wa. Hush! do you not hear the spirits talking? For your life, not a word!"

Pe-bo-a threw herself into an attitude of listening.

She was a devoted spiritualist, and evidently believed that she had the power at will of conversing with the denizens of the other world.

Olalla watched her curiously.

"Yes, yes!" she cried. "There is death in the air. Death! death!"

She waved her skinny arms in the air, and uttered low moans.

"What's the old fool up to?" asked Hunston.

Olalla told him the gist of the conversation, and Hunston affected to be incredulous.

"I don't know what there is about this fellow Harkaway," he said, "to frighten everybody. You look scared almost to death!"

"She great medicine!" replied Olalla, with a shake of the head.

"Great humbug!"

"Ah, there are things you don't understand—things in the earth, in the air. All mysteries."

"I know all I want to know," said Hunston.

"What's that?"

"Harkaway is up above. Let's go and capture him, put him in with the others. Pile up a heap of pine knots, and smother the whole lot."

"Good! good! if it can be done."

"I say it shall."

"May as well try, any how."

"Ask the old girl if she'll show us the way to the top."

"Plenty of time. Plenty daylight yet. Go now?"

"Certainly. It's no use waiting. I hate suspense."

"No good wait. You right"

"Of course I am. You see how easily we'll corner Harkaway. He's all alone. I long to have a go at him. Won't I make him quake and squeal, when he sees he has to die with his wife, his child, and his friends?"

"Good idea. Heap good," replied Olalla.

He spoke to Pe-bo-a who appeared somewhat reluctant to engage in the enterprise, but she admitted that her intended sacrifice on the morrow would be incomplete without Jack and after some persuasion she was induced to do as Hunston had suggested.

twice, and I must refer you to Hank for the knots."

"The knots, kernal, is two hills," said Hank. "There they are after the sights."

"And what distance is it altogether?"

"Which?" inquired Hank.

"Put it in miles. Simplify it."

"Wal, the sights is seven miles, the knots is three, and the get is a good five. Add that up."

"Fifteen in all."

"Now you've got it.

"That's enough to task the energies of a poor old man like me, with the rheumatism in one leg, a touch of sciatica, a suspicion of lumbago, and ——"

"Hold on, thar!" interrupted Hank. "If you say much more, we shall hev to send you to a hospital."

"Won't you let me off duty?"

"No, sir," replied Hank. "We want all hands. Work to-day, and we'll let you keep house to-morrow."

"I wish bears had never been invented," grumbled the Professor. "But at least, Harkaway," he added, "you will let me fill my little flask with some of that old bourbon you have stowed away in the waggon. The cask has a patent tap, and unless you give me the key, it merely tantalises the vision."

Harkaway tossed him the keys in a careless manner, and the Professor, calling Monday, walked to the waggon.

When the Malay joined him, he exclaimed—

"It's a very serious thing about Mrs. Harvey."

"Yes, sah!" exclaimed Monday.

"Couldn't have been robbers?"

"No robbers, sah, or else have taken all our stores, sah."

"Couldn't be Hunston and his gang?"

"No, sah; that's for sartin, Mist Mole, because they're all born thieves."

"What was it, then?"

"Not knowing, can't say."

"Where is she gone?"

"That's what's puzzling this child," said Monday.

"Well," continued the Professor, "suppose we take a little solid comfort?"

"Comfort is it, sah?"

"Yes."

"What's the name of um comfort?"

"Whisky!"

"Oh, golly, that's good!" said Monday; "I'm nigh froze to death, and that's a fact. You got um key, Mist Mole?"

"I have."

"Good for you."

"Who's your friend, Monday?"

"You am, sah."

"When I have good things don't I always put you in it?"

"Always, sah!"

"What do I care as long as two and two make four?"

"They don't always do that, sah."

"How?"

"Two and two make twenty-two. Ha! ha!"

"You're too smart for me," said Mr. Mole. "But I will finish my sentence. I mean to say that so long as the world lasts, I am the same old Mole. Jolly old Mole. They can't alter me."

"Go and fetch um bear to camp, sah."

"Hang the bear! Bother the bear! What are twelve bears to me? I want to take my ease. It isn't often I have a chance like this. Let us enjoy life while we can. We don't live long. Take another smile, Monday, and look pleasant. By jiminy! what a happy day we're having!"

He turned the tap again, and gave Monday another tin cupful of the potent spirit.

The black drank, and then coughed and sputtered.

"I thought I was um thoroughbred," he said; "but dat take my bref' way, Mist Mole."

"I feel kinder hiccuppy," replied the Professor. "I—hic—confound it, there must be something crooked about this whisky."

"That's what I'm thinking all um while, sah."

Their conversation was cut short by Harkaway's voice at the rear of the waggon.

"Rouse up, sir. Are you going to lounge in there all day?"

Mr. Mole raised his cloth and replied—

"Harkaway, I want you to know that you must not use improper language to me."

"Get out of that," replied Jack.

"I will not."

"You won't?"

"No, sir. I distinctly refuse. If you don't know when I have comfortable quarters, I do."

"That is all the return you make for giving you the key. I was a fool to do it."

"Of course you were. That is the first sensible remark you have made to-day."

"Give that key here."

"No, sir. I am master of the situation."

"But we want you to come after the bear."

"What is your bear to me?" replied Mr. Mole loftily.

"You are glad enough to eat the meat when you get it."

"Possibly; but, good gracious me," said the Professor, "two strong, hardy men like you and Hank are enough to haul home one poor bear and two mean little cubs."

"Come out."

"I will not."

Monday was standing up, and trying to look as if the whisky had not "bitten" him.

Jack caught his eye.

"Drag him out!" he exclaimed.

Monday caught Mole by the collar of his coat and urged him gently forward.

"Run 'way, sah. Me go with you," said Pete.

"Run?"

"Yes, sah."

"Where to?"

"Up to the mountains. Marse Hunston shoot you sure, when de woman get through with dying."

"I suppose he will," replied Jack.

"Dat's a fact, sure's you lib. Run mighty quick."

"But mamma?"

"Take her 'long wid us."

"All right."

"See here!" exclaimed Pete. "I've stole de rifles of de two Injuns, and two pair snow-shoes; got mine on. Hurry up, sah; put dem on!"

Young Jack obeyed mechanically.

"Injuns left deir rifles," continued Pete "Yah yah! Dis chile took a little tumble, and will be campin' to night on de ole cabin ground. Look at heah, Marse Jack, got bag ob powder, shot, anoder bag ob meat; dey's done gone fishing' an neber suspec' dis boy would do anything mean. Oh, no!"

Young Jack did not hesitate.

He put on the snow-shoes, grasped his rifle, the powder and meat, leaving the bullets to Pete.

"On, way, sah," said Pete.

He ran to where Viola was lying on the snow.

She was still insensible from the shock to the nervous system which the whipping had given her.

"Take up de legs, sah, and I take de head," said Pete.

They quickly lifted up the inanimate burden and were speedily running along the frozen snow, to the direction of the chain of hills which intersected the island.

It was hard work carrying Viola.

But they did not mind.

Pete was very faithful to them.

By his quickness and foresight he had made an effort to save their lives.

Probably he would be successful.

His common sense told him that when Hunston realised the fact of his loss he would become so furious that a bullet would probably be the portion of both Viola and Young Jack.

They had a good start.

Hunston did not think of them.

His thoughts were centred on Fannie, and when at length her spirit passed away, and the lovely face was cold and still, he sat by her side like one stupefied.

It was so awful!

So sudden!

For a moment he could not believe it true, but when the dreadful fact broke upon him with all its startling reality, he uttered loud cries of woe from the anguish of his bruised spirit; he called upon the Lord to take him too.

Then he threw himself upon her bosom and kissed her lips with fond affection.

Two hours passed.

He was aroused from his all-absorbing grief by the hand of Olalla.

"What mean this?" asked the chief, pointing to the dead body of Fannie.

Hunston sprang up.

He dashed the tear from his eyes, ashamed of his weakness.

"The boy did it!" he exclaimed. "Curse him, where is he?"

nowhere to be seen.

"Boy gone!" exclaimed Olalla, in his laconic manner.

"Gone!"

"Yes; while you weep over squaw, boy, woman, and black man go away."

"How do you know?"

"I look everywhere. Not here!"

"The deuce they are not! Then we must go after them."

"Very well. I come. Leave Indian here mind camp."

"Which way have they gone?"

"Easy to tell; leave trail; follow them up. Ugh!"

Olalla grunted as if this was only child's play to him.

"Start at once," said Hunston. "We can't bury my poor Fannie now; the ground is too hard. She's frozen stiff already, and will keep like that till a thaw comes."

"Put her in hut. Indian keep off bear, keep off cayote."

"Yes; that's the plan."

Hunston carried Fannie into the hut, and covered her with a skin.

His grief had worn off a little now.

Indeed his was too practical a nature to grieve much, and seeing that all the sorrow in the world would not bring her back to life, he turned his attention to punishing the boy, whom he falsely accused of being her murderer.

If he had not attacked Young Jack and tried to kill him, the former would not have struggled for possession of the pistol.

It was not his fault that the pistol went off.

The pistol did not belong to him.

He did not point the muzzle at Fannie's heart.

If anyone was guilty of murdering her, it was certainly Hunston himself.

"Now, are you ready for a start?" said Hunston.

"No!" exclaimed Olalla.

"Why not?"

"Tired, cold, got good fire, good fish. Want eat and sleep."

"Oh! I never care about eating or sleeping when I've got business on hand," exclaimed Hunston.

"Me do."

"Well, to oblige me, won't you hurry?"

"Make no difference," returned Olalla. "Not a darn bit."

"Why not? The boy will get away."

"No."

"I tell you he will. My prey will escape me, and I'll have his blood."

"That good enough. Have all blood want soon." said Olalla.

"H 'll give us the slip if we wait till morning. What a fool you are!"

"Me no fool!" said Olalla, calmly.

"How can we find them, with half a day and a whole night's start?"

"Very easy."

"Tell me."

"Can't escape his trail. Me find trail."

Hunston looked up in the sky.

"If you do, you're mighty clever," he said; "for it's beginning to snow, and the fresh snow will cover up their tracks and where will you be then?"

Olalla seemed somewhat disconcerted.

"Didn't think of fresh snow," he said.

"Of course you didn't."

utterly lost to the sight of the fast-fading winter's day.

Hunston and Olalla proceeded through an apparently interminable series of caverns, which quite undermined the hills for more than a mile.

Their wonder and admiration was excited by this spacious net work of caves.

They couldn't imagine where they terminated.

It seemed as if in certain places the hand of man had aided that of nature, though they could by no means be certain on that point.

Suddenly they saw a light.

It was small at first, but gradually grew brighter and stronger.

Grasping their weapons firmly, they advanced with caution.

They had been ascending an inclined plain for some time, and were apparently nearing the summit of a hill.

Probably this light, which was in no way artificial, proceeded from some fissure in the rock above.

At length they found themselves in a spacious vaulted chamber.

The light slanted down from a tunnel in the rock, and was refracted from its sides by means of a glittering species of mineral, resembling silver.

They paused.

Scarcely had they recovered their breath, which had been somewhat exhausted by climbing up the steep ascent, than they were confronted by an aged crone.

Her skin was red and her long hair hung in wiry mats over her body, which was destitute of clothing, save a roughly woven cloth, made of reeds, which was fastened over her shoulders and descended to her knees.

Though very old, she was lithe and vigorous, seeming to be in full possession of all her faculties.

Her gaze rested first on Hunston, and then on Olalla.

From the former she turned with a look of disgust; to the latter she extended a skeleton hand.

"You are a Bannock chief?" she exclaimed.

"I am the last of the Bannocks," he replied, drawing himself up proudly, "and I have never disgraced my name or nation. When the Great Spirit calls me, I am ready to go."

"This is a moon of death!" she exclaimed. "By signs that never failed me I know that you will soon go to the happy grounds where the good Indians hunt for ever, and no white man ever tread."

He bowed his head.

"Olalla is no coward; he is ready," was the answer.

"I am great medicine," she continued. "My signs told me that a great chief of the Indian nation would come here to die. It's fitting that he should meet his fate in the sacred Kehamas."

"Are you Pe-bo-a?"

"He knows me. The tradition of the tribes do not deceive. My name lives among my people."

"Many years have you lived here?" said Olalla.

"One thousand two hundred moons have passed over my head," she replied.

Reckoning twelve moons to a year—that is, one each month, this calculation would make her a hundred years old.

As far as her weird appearance went, she might have been two hundred, though she was singularly active and vigorous for her age.

"I have lived in the Kehamas fifty years," she went on, "and fled here after a massacre of my tribe by the white men. I have sworn that I would let no white man live, and I have now revenge within my grasp."

The conversation was carried on in the Indian tongue, and was not understood by Hunston, who, however, through living among the redskins, had picked up a few words, which, nevertheless, did not render her remarks intelligible to him.

"How—how?" said Olalla.

"I have prisoners," she replied. "One white woman, three white men, and one black one, and to-day I captured another black man, a white man, and a white boy. In camp over our heads one more white man. When I have him, I will kill all."

"All?"

"Yes. To-morrow they die."

Olalla mused over this news.

Who could Pe-bo-a's captives be?

Turning to Hunston he said—

"She tells me she is going to have a massacre of prisoners to-morrow."

"Hope she won't kill us," replied Hunston.

"How could she? We are armed. Besides, I am the last of the Bannocks, and one of her own people."

"That's true."

"We are safe," said Olalla.

"Ask who her prisoners are?"

Turning to the aged crone again, Olalla exclaimed—

"Did you not know my father?"

"You call yourself Olalla?" she answered.

"Yes."

"Your mother was Ge-ha-ha?"

"Yes. That was her name."

"Know, then, that I am your mother's sister, Olalla, and you are my blood relation"

"Good. It is well," said Olalla. "O, Pe-bo-a, my heart warms toward you!"

"I have had dreams," she continued. "Your coming was foretold me, and I fear my end is approaching, but I shall have blood before I die. Blood of the hated white man. Ha! ha!"

She laughed with a fiendish glee till her elfin locks shook.

"How have you lived here?" he asked.

She pointed to the tunnel-like shaft through which the light which illumined the cavern descended.

"That is a pit which in old times communicated with the fires of earth. It is still now. A few feet, and you come to the surface. I have cut steps in the rock. I climb up. One false step, and you are dashed to atoms in the abyss. I have a bow. I have arrows. I kill game. The Great Spirit is good, and Pe-bo-a does not require much to sustain life."

"Let us see your captives," said Olalla.

Pe-bo-a walked a few paces, and pushed aside a rock which barred egress from a small cave, the dimensions of which were scarcely bigger than that of the famous Black Hole of Calcutta.

In it were the prisoners she had spoken of.

Hunston flashed his pine-knot in their faces.

They were all bound with strong withes, and seemed to be suffering much from thirst, hunger, and confinement.

"Water! water!" feebly moaned one.

"Ha!" cried Hunston. "You have made a fine haul?"

Pe-bo-a pushed the stone back, and shut up the miserable wretches in their prison-pen once more.

In Harkaway's rear was the pleasant little settlement of Flyaway Gap, whose r dely-built frame houses gleamed white in the noonday sun.

Under his mask of ease, Hunston was evidently unnerved.

He had become deathly pale.

His hand clutched his rifle in a nervous grasp.

But he made no attempt to raise its butt from the sand on which it was resting.

"Lo k here," said Jack. "I know you hate me, and have sworn to kill me, so what's the use of talking about being friends?"

"I'd like to be," replied Hunston. "Here have I wandered to this island after escaping from Atewe-an-pe, and finding Olalla and all my friends dead or scattered. Why can't I enter your camp and be one of you?"

"Impossible."

"Oh, that's not your usual style, Harkaway. There used to be nothing mean about you."

"There is now."

"Why?"

"Because you hired two men to drown me."

"I?"

Hunston spoke in a tone of feigned astonishment, and his surprise was so well simulated it would not have disgraced a veteran actor.

"Yes. Did you never meet Spanish Joe?"

"Never."

"Nor a fellow called Gosh?"

"No, indeed."

"As God's your judge?"

"I've told you no," replied Hunston, sulkily.

"You won't swear?" said Jack. "Not that it matters much if you would. I know you Hunston, and I have had quite enough of your persecution."

"If Gosh, as you call him, says I hired him to drown you, bring him face to face with me."

"I can't."

"How's that?"

"He's dead—killed by my hand to-day."

"Well, bring the other one."

"He's shot in the leg by Harvey, and is lying hid in the woods."

"It's very odd you can't bring your witnesses," said Hunston. "Those fellows may have tried to drown you for your money and valuables. There are desperate men on this ranche, and if they say I had anything to do with it, they are playing on you."

"It's odd you should be around here."

"Why? I am a wanderer, and want to find some place to settle down for a while."

"And you didn't want to kill me?"

"No, Harkaway."

"Don't you now?"

Hunston's lips moved.

He was saying to himself—

"I only wish I had the chance."

But he exclaimed—

"Let bygones be bygones. Give me another chance, and see if I won't behave well."

"Shall I tell you a little story?" asked Jack, with a bitter smile'

"If you like."

"One day a man dug up a snake in the ground. It was winter time, and the snake was frozen hard. He took it home, and placed it before the fire. In two hours that reptile thawed out, and then it tried to bite him."

"Is this," replied Jack. "If I take you by the hand now, I shall be sure to suffer for it in the future."

"You won't trust me?"

"No further than I can see you.'

A gleam of hatred, of defiance, almost of scorn, flashed a hwart his fair face.

All the fiend within him was rising to the surface.

"Well," he exclaimed fearlessly, "let us throw off this disguise."

"As soon as you like."

"I'm ready."

"And I like to meet a man in his true colours."

"I hate you," said Hunston.

"And you have sworn to kill me to avenge your brother's death, you one-eyed fraud," said Jack.

"Don't call me that," said Hunston, with a quick, short gasp.

"I shall call you just what I choose."

"You made me lose my sight of the left eye."

"How?"

"Anyway, if the Indians did it, you were the cause of it, by bringing me to the village"

"No matter. Go on with business," said Jack. "You hired those two men to kill me?"

"I did."

"That's something. Own up like a man."

"I'm not afraid to."

"So it appears."

"You see I don't scare worth a cent,"

"More shame for you. Now tell me," said Jack, "what reason there is that I shouldn't shoot you down like a dog?"

"A very good one," responded Hunston, with a harsh laugh.

"Name it."

"So soon as you raised your gun, I'd hoist mine, and perhaps you'd scratch grass first."

"That's so; but I'm quick, and my aim is sure."

"So is mine. Try it."

Jack hesitated.

At this moment he was seized from behind.

Something grasped his legs, jerked him down, and he fell on his back.

In an instant Hunston sprang forward.

He precipitated himself upon Harkaway like an avalanche.

Kneeling on his chest, he presented his pistol at his ear.

"Stir hand or foot," he said, "and you are a dead man!"

Jack was overwhelmed

Never was surprise so complete

What could it be?

"Ha, ha, ha!" chuckled a voice behind him. It was Spanish Joe.

The villain, faithful to his employer, and enraged at the death of Gosh, had tracked Harkaway as well as his wounded leg would permit him.

Jack never once looked behind him when going to the rendezvous at the Giant's Rock.

He was too intent on meeting Hunston, and wiping out old scores with him.

"It is easy to see with half an eye that you know no more about seamanship than a pig does about deer-stalking, therefore the inference is that you are land-lubbers.

"Now, I am positive that no one lent you this boat, so you must have come by it dishonestly"

"That don't stand to reason at all, master," replied Spanish Joe. "We're pals with all the boys at the Gap."

"Let that pass. What have you done with the man?"

"What man?" asked Joe, assuming a look of profound astonishment.

"The man I heard screaming for help a short time ago."

"You must have been dreaming. We've no man on board, and never had. You've fancied it, guv'nor, or else you heard the gulls screeching and thought it was a man. You can see into our boat well enough. Use your eyes and look, and if you see anything in the shape of a man, why, I'll forgive you for trying to take away an honest man's character."

The stranger looked carefully into the boat.

While he was so engaged, Spanish Joe leant over and made a snatch at the gun, which was lying within tempting distance of the fellow's hand.

But its owner, with great rapidity, brought his fist down on the man's arm, with a violence which made him howl again.

"That will teach you not to meddle with things that do not belong to you," the stranger remarked, with a quiet smile of satisfaction. "That serves you right; now with regard to the man. Have you made away with him?"

"Is it likely, now," said Joe, with an assumption of innocence which did not belong to him—"is it likely that we should touch any one to hurt him? Of course it isn't. We don't do things like that, sir, where we came from. It's no use your looking any further, squire. You're mistaken, and you'd better go your way while we go ours."

During this reply, Joe had rubbed his arm with a lugubrious air, for the blow he had received hurt him considerably.

The stranger was one of those iron-fisted men who, when they do put themselves out of the way to strike another one, hit like sledge-hammers.

Had not the ruffian's arm been made of good material, it would have snapped in half like a piece of rotten stick beneath the force of the blow.

Gosh had not uttered a word.

He left the oratorical department entirely in his confederate's hands, contenting himself with sitting upon the locker, so as to repel with force of arms any attempt to approach that locality.

"I could have sworn that I was not mistaken," said the stranger, who appeared to be puzzled, "but as you assure me that you had no one on board, and as I can see nothing to lead me to disbelieve that statement, I suppose I must sheer off and let you go."

"You shouldn't be so hasty, boss," said Spanish Joe. "It's a bad plan to suspect honest folks. Some mightn't have taken it so quietly as we have done. Don't you do it no more, guv'nor; that's my advice to you"

Just as the stranger was about to withdraw his boat-hook, a cry proceeded from the region of the locker.

"Ha!" cried the stranger. "At last fortune has so far favoured your victim as to allow him, in his own proper person, to give the lie to your assertions He is confined in some locker you have in the after-part of the boat. Produce him this instant, or the consequences will be what you will strongly disapprove of."

"If you want him, you had better get him yourself," said Spanish Joe, surlily.

"I shall do nothing of the sort. Disobey me at your peril my good fellow. I am not a man to be trifled with, and in the cause of humanity I would as soon put a charge of shot in your worthless carcase as look at you.

When Joe found that there was no escape, he made a virtue of necessity, and said to Gosh:—

"Let the varmint out. It's hard enough."

Gosh undid the door of the locker and allowed Jack to crawl out.

He gazed around him curiously for a few seconds, and then made a spring into the stranger's boat.

The stranger promptly cut the rope which tied his hands.

The next moment their hands were clasped in a firm grasp.

"Dick!"

"Jack!"

The stranger was Dick Harvey, who had come up in time to rescue his old friend.

Five minutes more, and he would have been too late.

Bound as he was, Jack must have sunk in a short space, if he had been thrown into the lake.

"Thank God!" said Harvey.

"So say I," said Jack

"How did this happen?"

"I'll tell you presently."

"Now, you fellows, sheer off," exclaimed Harvey, "or I'll warm you. If I see you at the Gap, I'll put the Select Men on to you, no fear; so you'd best skip from here, and choose new territory. Sail off! Hurry."

The two men sullenly acquiesced in this proposal.

They sat down, resigned to their fate, and smoked their pipes in a lethargic manner.

Spanish Joe hoisted the sail, and the two boats separated.

"Look here, my good fellow," continued Harvey. "I don't know what your motive may have been in endeavouring to injure my friend, but I should strongly advise you not to attempt a repetition of your dastardly conduct, for I shall not be inclined next time to let you off so easily as I have done to-day."

When Spanish Joe found himself at a safe distance, he said—

"I've something to say to you, master, and you'd best bear it in mind. If it should so happen that either me or my pal comes across you on a dark night, you may say your prayers, for it will be all over with you."

Harvey raised his gun to his shoulder, and, taking a careful aim, fired, putting part of the contents of one barrel in Joe's right leg.

He was too far off for the shot to do him any severe injury, but the half-dozen shot that entered his flesh made him cry out with pain.

"That is something for you to remember me

"I, Metamora, have said it.

"Written in the blood of the dying chief on the prepared skin of a beast by the aforesaid Manuel Quesada."

Then followed, in small letters:

"In nomine Patri, Filii et Spiritus Sanctus.

"† Amen. †"

Jack's countenance fell when he read this.

All his hope of sudden and enormous wealth vanished, as had that of many others who had gone to the Black Hills to get rich in a hurry.

"Read it out, Jack!" said Harvey.

"Read it yourself!" he exclaimed.

"Is it the Secret of Wealth?"

"Yes!" said Jack, drily.

"Where is the Mountain of Gold?"

"In yourself!"

"Don't chaff! I mean what is the Secret of Wealth?"

"Read for yourself, I say," was all the reply Harkaway made.

Harvey took the scroll and read it attentively.

When he had finished the perusal of this unique document, he burst into a loud fit of laughter.

"What a confounded sell!" he exclaimed.

Jack had had time to reflect.

"Not so much of a sell, after all," he replied. "Men follow shadows all their lives, and, like the dog in the fable, neglect the substance. Old Metamora was right. I guess we'll make tracks for home."

"And give up our Mountain of Gold?"

"Yes, sir!"

"Well," said Harvey, "perhaps that's the best thing we can do. The men at the Gap are only making a living, if they are doing that."

Pensively they retraced their steps, taking the manuscript of the monk with them.

Manuel Quesada had not thrown his pearls before those who were not likely to take notice of them.

His precepts sank deep into the minds of all, and when Harkaway's friends heard them, they agreed that they were worth more than mine riches.

Mr. Mole observed—

"It comes rather late at my time of life, but those are the doctrines I have all along observed."

"Give the professor a drink," said Young Jack, with a laugh.

Harkaway remained a month in camp, till the snow melted, and then retraced his steps to the Gap.

He abandoned his idea of finding the Mountain of Gold.

The legend current among the Indians as to its existence was sufficiently well explained now.

He thanked Harkaway for his kindness, but would make no terms with him.

"It is war between us wherever we meet," he exclaimed.

"So be it," said Jack.

Harkaway and his friends departed for New York, leaving Hunston at Flyaway Gap.

Whether they would ever meet again was a problem.

Jack cared very little whether they did or not.

After several weeks of weary travelling, they reached Cheyenne City and proceeded to New York.

Jack bought a large house, with farm land attached, in the County of Worcester, where Hank, Mo day, Harvey and Hilda took up their abode with him

Viola was very happy now.

She would often say to Young Jack, who was learning to become a practical farmer—

"Now, I have no trouble."

"Wait till the old man takes a fit in his head to travel again," said the Cheerful.

"Don't mention it. I hope he never will. I've had enough of Indians"

"Perhaps he'll take us to India next in search of the Koh-i-Noor, or explore Ceylon for a white elephant."

Harkaway had entered the room during these remarks.

With a smile, he said:—

"You are wrong my boy. My occupation just now is farming."

"That is mine, too, pop," said Young Jack.

"Yours will be altered soon."

"How?"

"I am going to send you to college."

"What college?"

"You'll know when the time comes."

"That's bully!" said young Jack. "I'll be a rowing man, and win all the races."

"You'll be a reading man," said his father.

"I'll be a little of both," said the Cheerful.

Viola looked at Harkaway and smiled.

"He will never disgrace our name," she said; "of that I am sure."

"No," replied Jack. "He knows the Secret of Wealth, which cost me so much danger and difficulty to learn, and that's as good as a fortune for a young man in his start in life"

*   *   *   *   *

Here ends our story, and it is yet possible that our old friend Harkaway, or our young friend Jack, may be heard from again, when they have recovered from the fatigues and perils of their search after the "Secret of Wealth."

THE END.